Running Wild Anthology of Stories

Volume 3

Edited by Cecile Sarruf

Published in North America and Europe by Running Wild Press. Visit Running Wild Press at www.runningwildpress.com Educators, librarians, book clubs (as well as the eternally curious), go to www.runningwildpress.com for teaching tools.

ISBN (pbk) 978-1-947041-30-1
ISBN (ebook) 978-1-947041-38-7

Printed in the United States of America.

Contents

Clara Came to St. Mary's

By Hailey Piper

She came *to St. Mary's Orphanage for Girls* on September 3rd, 1948. I remember the first time I saw her pale yellow dress, before she hid things beneath the hem. It was the day Sister Agnes bled little Jane's fingertips during needlework for stealing. Jane didn't want to steal, just felt she had to, but none of us dared explain that to Sister Agnes. We would only be punished, too. She pricked seven of Jane's fingers, one for each needle.

Clara was annoying from the start. Little choppy-haired creature never once called me by name, always "wee girl" from a sprout who stood a head shorter than me.

There wasn't much odd about her that first day, maybe not even that week. She sat in lessons with us, cleaned with us, sewed with us, listened to Mother Caroline read the Bible, which, we were told, was a special treat. Clara was quiet then. She only spoke when spoken to, her peepers wide as the ocean, drinking up everything about the orphanage, the sisters, and the rest of us.

It wasn't until one night, with Beth, that things changed. She was a whisperer, we all were, but Beth wasn't a sneaky whisperer. She didn't know how to talk in a way where she was still listening for the sisters. We were in the big bedroom, each wall lined with our little cots. Beth was chattering away to no one in particular about a doll's hair when Sister Grace burst through the door and squared in on

Beth like she could tell one of our whispers apart from any other.

She locked one hand under Beth's chin and squeezed her cheeks. "You see the rest of them? All down in prayer, the same way we put you to bed, in case the Lord should need take you in the night. And here you are, sitting up, chattering. It's devil talk." She let go of Beth's chin and swung the back of her hand against that little face. Beth fell onto the bed, clutching her cheek. I remember blood, but I can't imagine how I'd seen any in the dark.

"You lie with hands clasped," Sister Grace said. "Let the pain remind you of your sin. The rest of you, to sleep." She swept out fast as she came and snapped the door shut behind.

Clara's cot lay next to mine. Not long after Sister Grace left us, Clara turned to me and whispered, "So that's how it is here?"

I wouldn't say a word in case the sister prowled the door, but I nodded, not that Clara should've seen in the dark.

She seemed to, as she said, "So it is." Then she rolled over, and we went to sleep.

From then on, I spotted Clara wearing boy's clothes, some old brown shirt and a pair of brown shorts she must have found outside. Sometimes she hid them under her dress, other times she wore them while the sisters weren't looking. No one would tell. You never knew in those days, what was secretly a sin. It seemed a game to Clara, how long she could get away with flaunting her boy's clothes before one of the sisters popped around the corner.

She would even dance in those shorts, her skinny legs crooked at the knees. We only stared. I felt a little laugh in the back of my throat, but swallowed it. Giggling was a sin. This went on for some time without a single sister having seen her. She even wore the shirt and shorts to bed. Sometimes she slept naked.

One night, I felt a finger poke between my shoulders. Clara knelt between our cots.

"What?"

"Sweets, wee girl." Clara's tiny fist bloomed into a white paper, wrapped around a chewy piece of candy.

There in the dark, I didn't know how she found candy. It was a sweet, which we rarely tasted. There was no reason to deny myself. I never asked if she only gave candy to me, or if there was a piece for every girl in the bedroom. What I know is that I was the only girl the sisters caught.

It was my mistake. I left the candy's paper on the floor, where Sister Grace snatched it up. I wouldn't tell who gave it, said I found it somewhere, but she told me it was stolen from Mother Caroline. She reminded me it was a sin to lie, a sin to steal, and each sin was worth five lashes with a leather strap. Then it was a sin to cry, and I got five more. Clara inspected my back that night. She said the wounds would heal, but not the scars. "My fault, wee girl."

"Would you not call me that?" I asked. "I'm a head taller than you."

"Wee not in size, but in years," she said, but I was eight and she couldn't have been any older. Her fingers were tender on my skin, but the lashes ached for days.

After that, Clara grew bolder. She flashed her boy's clothes in front of Sister Joan, who grabbed her and yanked up her dress, only to find nothing underneath. Another time, she did the same to Sister Grace, only without the dress to hide beneath. The sisters chased her round one corner in boy's clothes, only to find her back in the dress when they caught up with her. I swear sometimes she passed me and there was a boy's face beneath her choppy short hair that never seemed to grow, other times a girl. There was no telling even on the day Sister Grace grasped Clara by the arm and stripped the shirt and shorts off her hide in front of everyone in the dining hall. She was a boy at that moment. I saw so myself. Sister Grace looked like she'd seen a ghost.

Clara just smirked in that crooked way I came to know as hers. "Why Sister Grace, I didn't know we could runs naked in this place. What a paradise!" She hopped off the table and bolted down the hall.

Sister Grace chased her, caught her wrist. "How did you hide you're a boy?"

But when she whirled naked Clara around, there was only a girl standing there. Innocent and wide-eyed, she asked, "What's wrong, sister? Think you seen something you been missing all your life?"

When Sister Grace dragged Clara away, I knew they were headed for the narrow closet. I had been there once. It was an uncomfortable slit in the wooden wall. The ceiling leaned down and away from the door, barely space to stand, but the sides were too tight to really lie down or sit. Most girls came out aching, hungry, exhausted. Some had wet themselves. That was the first time Clara was thrown in the narrow closet, but not the last. I'll never forget the last.

They let her out a day later, and it was as if Sister Grace had made a mortal enemy. Not that anyone saw Clara do anything. Only, I noticed things didn't seem to go Sister Grace's way anymore. She would prick her own fingers during needlework or trip up stairs she'd climbed over a thousand times. Her bread was often soggy or stale, and she and Sister Joan nearly came to blows over bread slices once, before Sister Agnes settled them.

Somehow she found a way to blame Clara, who never went more than a couple of weeks without visiting the narrow closet. She never seemed to have too hard a time, and maybe the sisters guessed it was because she was so small. Perhaps her size saved her from worse punishments.

I admired her boldness enough to grow bolder myself. We inched our cots closer together at night, little enough that if one of the sisters stalked inside to inspect, they wouldn't notice in the gloom, but it made all the difference to us that we could hold each other's hands and whisper a little more quietly so as not to be heard. In that darkness, we confided in each other. I told her my parents left me at the orphanage when I was six, said they'd be back someday. That was the last I ever saw them.

Clara said she never had any parents. She said grew in dark places, like a mushroom. She told me that a priest once tried to baptize her, but she swallowed all the baptismal water in one gulp, not spilling a drop.

We swapped our secrets and also the secrets of the sisters. How Sister Elise had grown fat for a few months, and then one day she was thin. How Sister Joan hid dirty magazines behind a loose floor plank. How none of the sisters, and not even Mother Caroline, would visit the attic alone. I came to believe something terrible once happened up there, worse than all the beatings and lashings and starving I'd witnessed.

"Something terrible lives there," Clara said, and I didn't ask how she knew. I believed her. "Stay away, wee girl."

Three days later, Clara pushed Sister Grace too hard. Sister Joan couldn't fetch the milk bottle on high that morning. She wouldn't leave the washroom. Many times I'd seen her at the sink basin, scrubbing her hands so rough, her fingers bled, as if there was a sin beneath her skin that she couldn't wash away.

Sister Grace came to the kitchen to fetch the milk bottle. Clara stood next to me then, as she had taken to doing. I felt her trembling beside me, like she was holding in the biggest laughter, and knew something was about to happen that made Clara proud. The bottle tipped over a glass to be poured, but a surprise weight dragged it out of Sister Grace's hand. Both bottle and glass fell to the floor, shattering, and a hundred white marbles spilled free across the kitchen, around our feet, into the hall. Not one of us ran to collect them, not even filch one for fun later. It would be an admission of guilt.

Clara hopped onto the table, as if the marbles were white mice, and yanked up her dress to show off her shirt and shorts. "Oh, thank me lards above, Sister Grace, you found me marbles! I feared I'd lost them, I did!" Knees crooked, Clara danced a little jig to Sister Grace's horror.

We couldn't help it. Giggling broke through the group, and then we quickly stifled ourselves. I bit my cheeks not to laugh, only for a snort to escape louder than the giggles.

Laughing was a sin. Dancing was a sin. Marbles were probably a sin. I don't know what dancing to marbles and making little girls laugh is, but Sister Grace took it for a sin. She grabbed Clara by the scruff of her scalp and hauled her off the table. When she near tripped on a marble, another hushed cloud of giggling ran through the girls. Sister Grace didn't even look at us. There was no chastising, no lecture. Silent, she dragged Clara down the hall, into the narrow closet, where she locked her and left her.

I expected she'd be freed the next morning, but Sister Grace never stepped near the door. For a second night, I went to bed without Clara's hand to hold and whispers to hear. And then a third. Sometimes I awoke in the dark hours and thought there was a shape beneath the blankets of Clara's cot, larger than any of the sisters. It breathed slow and cumbersome, loud as a bear. By morning, the blankets would be empty. Clara was still in the narrow closet.

The sisters didn't bring her food or water. For all I knew, Sister Grace alone was aware there was a child locked away. I tried to bring her water in a little cup, which I meant to spill so that it ran under the doorway, but Sister Grace caught my arm before I could make it. She gave me a lashing, wouldn't tell me why.

"But she'll die!"

"What would you know, little devil?"

I knew three days without water was death. And death for a

sinning child such as Clara was Hell.

I think the sisters forgot about her, or pretended to. There was a peace among them without Clara's being around to prance in boy's clothes or make Sister Grace stub her toe on corners, if Clara could somehow be blamed for that.

It wasn't until Jane was caught with a piece of bread she'd hidden away that they remembered. Sister Grace caught her sneaking it a week after the milk bottle incident and pulled her by the arm to the narrow closet. Why one of us might be bled, another lashed, another locked up, all for similar sins, I never knew. But I was there when Sister Grace opened the door to the narrow closet, ready to stuff Jane inside. I heard Sister Grace shriek.

There was Clara, no thirstier, no hungrier, not even any dirtier than when she'd been thrown in seven days before. Sister Grace let go of Jane and marched away.

I hugged Clara hard and cried harder. "How?"

Clara only smirked. "I wasn't in there long, wee girl. Only stepped from the day they shut the door to the day they opened it. Easy trick, you see."

That evening, I overheard Sister Grace's shouting through the door of Mother Caroline's room. "If it does something wrong, get Sister Agnes, Sister Elise, I don't care. I'm not touching that *thing* again!"

Some days, I think that should've been the end of the whole orphanage. The sisters were outwitted. Why should they be allowed to taunt and beat us? Why should they decide sin?

Clara's boldness was infectious. I wanted to see Sister Joan's secret. We all knew where the board was, but none ever dared look. I waited until Sister Joan had taken to one of her washing tortures and then I pried the board off. There were magazines, most of them scrunched or rolled. Each of them hid black and white photographs of naked people inside. The sisters said to be naked was a sin, but everyone was naked sometimes, so I couldn't understand what was so dirty about these.

A claw grasped my shoulder, wheeled me around to Sister Joan, face red as an apple. "Where did you get these? How did you get this filth inside our holy home?"

I didn't know what to say. Sister Joan muttered something to Sister Agnes, while I tried to get the words out. Not mine. They were yours. The sisters each took me by one arm and dragged me upstairs. We were nearly there before I understood where they were taking me, and by then all I could do was scream. I'd have done anything they wanted, let them do anything they wanted, just so they wouldn't put me up there.

They threw open the attic door. The place was a cavern, black as the deepest pits, and it only grew deeper the longer you looked at its darkness. There was nothing up there that you could see from the trapdoor, except a steel chair, trimmed with leather straps. Sister Joan strapped me in. Sister Agnes looked back and forth, as if standing watch.

Then they left me.

My screaming went on until I was hoarse. I rocked back and forth until I'd nearly thrown the chair over, but I didn't want to lie on the floor. Somehow that would make it worse. Soon I was in tears. I thought maybe if I sobbed loud enough, they would come back and take me to be lashed. Crying was a sin.

Night set in. Blackness became absolute. I heard things around me and hoped they were only mice. Clara had told me something terrible lived up here. I didn't want to know it. I wanted to eat supper and use the bathroom, to sleep in our cots beside each other and whisper about what I had found that day. A voice emerged in the dark. It asked me a question. "What do you get when you cross a country with a bomb?" I looked around, but there was nothing to see. "An explanation." It was Clara. Choppy-haired, runty Clara.

"How did you get up here?"

"Wee girl, I know darkness like this."

The blackness blinded me, but I felt Clara's presence as if her hand hung only inches from mine.

"Will you let me out?"

"I can't. But I want you to hear this. It's important. Are you ready?"

I was. I shut my mouth and listened.

"What kind of cake do you make with twenty clams?" I swear her smirk made a sound. "A stomach ache. Now you tell me one."

"It's too dark. How am I supposed to laugh when it's this dark?"

"Wee girl, there's always too much dark. You must keep your sense of humor, else you'll end up like them below. Your time here is near an end. If you can't think up your own, repeat after me. What do you get when you cross a potato with an elephant? Mashed potatoes."

I repeated it. Maybe even giggled a little.

We went on like that through the night. Some moments, the blackness became solid, a terrible presence that stared into my eyes, unseeing. Clara was always bigger, louder, closer to me. The darkness never brightened, but it thinned. Sometimes I laughed at her jokes, even the really stupid ones. Especially the really stupid ones.

I think, before Clara came, had I seen the sisters, Grace or Agnes or Joan or Elise, even Mother Caroline, brandish cleavers and slaughter one of the girls, and then cook her up and serve her to us for supper, I wouldn't have said a word. It would have been a silent supper, feasting on one of our own, terrified that the first to speak might be next. Not after Clara, though. She saw me through to morning, when the attic's darkness lifted just a little and Sister Joan and Sister Agnes returned to release me.

They found me dry-eyed and smiling. "Back so soon? I'd like to stay longer."

Their faces were chalk white with confusion.

"Before you go, I need to tell you something I learned up here. Why did the groom choose bread for his best man?" I smiled wider for them. "It makes the best toast."

Papers were put in order to transfer me to a secular home, noting disturbed behavior. Really, the sisters had decided if the attic couldn't unmake me, then I was out of control. I waved to Clara from the car window, the closest we came to a goodbye. She was still smirking that way she liked. I was adopted soon thereafter.

St. Mary's Orphanage for Girls shut down two months later. Nothing in the newspaper said exactly why, only that the sisters decided they couldn't care for the girls anymore. They could pretend it was their idea, but Clara was to blame. To thank. The sisters couldn't unmake me, but she had unmade them.

I'm old now. I've been old for awhile, I think. The years have given me two children and five grandchildren. I think about them every day, and when I watch them play, my memory falls to St. Mary's. The little girls won't ever end up there, but tell that to the attic in my mind. These nightmares don't go away. Sometimes it's a surprise even to me. After so many years, still angry? Yes, even anger that's weathered and ancient like me, may still fester inside. If I didn't release it, I'd die with it in my heart. There are things that happened inside that place, which I won't say, and probably more things forever lost to time.

Last night, I drove out to the orphanage. The building had been put to use one way or another over the decades, but it's never been consistent since the sisters shut it down. I drove there with two canisters of gasoline nestled in the trunk. If I'm to be old and die someday, I'd see that building die first and maybe all those memories, too. But not of Clara. Those were to keep.

I found her standing outside, as if she had been waiting for me all these years. Nothing about her had changed, not her eyes, not her hair, not her yellow dress or the shirt and shorts beneath. I lugged the two canisters of gasoline and laid them at her feet. "How?"

"Got here same as always, wee girl. I stepped from the day you left and into the day you came back. Easy trick." Then she smirked the way she always did.

We poured the gasoline together. My gnarled hands were shaking so hard, I almost dropped the match, but she held them still enough so that the flame went where it was supposed to go. And then, once the doorway was alight, Clara took a cloud of the fire into her hands and ran into the orphanage. Up the stairs, down the halls, into the bedroom and the dining hall and Sister Joan's room — where she hid her magazines. Clara threw the fire into the attic too, where maybe it could burn the terrible thing that lived there. She did it all laughing and running and dancing, each a sin, but this last night at St. Mary's, the joy of sin ran free.

Author's Bio:

Hailey Piper is a speculative writer whose short fiction has appeared in publications such as SERIAL Magazine and Neon Druid. She grew up in a patch of creepy American woods that filled her imagination with Bigfoot and ghosts, and today she keeps those childhood fantasies alive by writing them down. Her debut novella, The Haunting of Natalie Glasgow, was released in October 2018.

Los Sueños

By Dawn DeAnna Wilson

The dead made it possible for Flora to dream again. She had stopped months ago. Her dreams had become weak like worn burlap, come apart piece by piece, until nothing was left but long scraps of mismatched threads. Her dreams vanished like a cobweb stretched too far, breaking into silvery, misty strands. Sleep without dreams didn't nourish her; it left her weak-willed, depressed and exhausted.

Eighty-hour work weeks demanded that residents caught rest whenever possible: cat nap here and there, a few hours before next shift. Without dreams, Flora's hollow slumber drained her mind until her sieve – like memory allowed muscle groups, dosages, treatment protocols and other priceless information to pass through her brain unrestrained, flow downward and trail away from her.

After her surgery rotation, her specialty choices grew dangerously thin. Lethargic, she almost blacked out during an appendectomy. She carried the undercurrent of sneers from her colleagues. She heard whispers throughout the hallways.

"Labor and delivery? Don't send Flora—she'll fall asleep and drop the poor baby on its head."

"Psychiatry? She's half-crazy herself."

"Surgery? No one wants a repeat of the appendectomy episode."

"ER? No. Oh God, no."

She was relieved when she started her pathology rotation, where she could do no harm. The patients didn't complain, and tissue samples didn't criticize her bedside manner.

Her father was mortified. "You go to school to help the living mija, not to tend the fields of the dead! Who would marry a woman who reeks of formaldehyde? Dios mio."

Her mind was thirsty for dreams, but Flora resigned herself to fate. She would never dream again. The third day of her pathology rotation changed that. She experienced the dreams of the dead. She was alone in the morgue. From the corner of her eye, she saw a narrow glowing yellow strand that looked like yarn wrapped around the handle of one of the cold chambers. She grasped it; it was thin and strong, like fishing wire. When she unraveled it, the strand dissolved into her fingertips. She took the handle of the cold chamber and pulled at it slowly.

His tag said he was 28. Javier Ortiz. She traced every inch of his pale skin with her gaze, gently pausing on the large "Y," a blessing from the pathologist, marked across his chest. Next of kin had yet to be notified. She gingerly touched the soft spot on his forehead between his eyebrows and it was then that she felt him dreaming. Like a cold rain, it burst into her mind and exploded with a thousand colors she didn't know existed. Dreams of the dead were as if soaked in heavy Technicolor silver-sprinkled bliss. Dreams of the dead were intoxicating and liberating, full of deep lavender memories and lemon-kissed joy.

His dream. His eyes: a vision of apple trees unfurling before her. There was an orchard just outside of Hendersonville where they were gathering large, red, delicious orbs into buckets. He was helping Antonio, the smallest one, hoisting him upon willing shoulders so his tiny hands could venture forth and pick one. He had difficulty at first—- the branch did not want to let go of its sweet treasure. He gestured to Antonio—You have to twist your wrist, like this. Antonio did, and took his apple. Antonio was so proud that day.

The orchard faded and she was in the middle of a warm kitchen filled with the scent of fresh apple pie. Joy and love washed over her 'till she felt herself floating, slowly rising to the ceiling. She had a thousand questions burning through her mind:

Where is your family?

Who is Antonio?

Does anyone know you're here?

But the dream demanded her to be quiet. It insisted that she drink in and savor these images. Like wine running through water, it transformed her. Sleep was restful.

The pathologist was not pleased.

"The dead don't dream. You have narcolepsy," he said. "I came back and you were slouched in the chair. Snoring, even. Get a sleep study. See a doctor."

"Who is he?" She asked.

"Don't ask if they don't belong to you."

"Have you ever heard them dream? Have you seen the glowing thread?"

"It's a dangerous thing to take dreams that aren't yours."

The next day another golden thread appeared, Flora followed it to a cold chamber, untied it, and opened the chamber to an old black woman — dentures removed, lips curled inward. Flora gently touched her forehead, as if afraid the lady would awake. When her finger met the mocha flesh, her senses exploded onto a hot, sweltering afternoon. The woman was desperately cooling herself with a cardboard fan that had a pictorial of Jesus on one side and a coupon from Dales Tire and Auto on the other. The woman's Nikki was up front belting a tune to make the angels cry. Then the woman was soaring. Soaring and floating over a pink Alabama sunset.

The next day, another thread. A blond teenager fantasized about her dream job, home, family, children and grandchildren.

Another thread brought her to a fifty-year-old man with lung cancer. He breathed the cold, thin air of Denali, his spiked crampons stabilized his boots as he climbed across miles of ice.

Yet another — this time, a small child who only dreamed of kittens.

But, she always found her way back to Javier. His dreams were the most beautiful and delicate. Making homemade tomato soup with vegetables from his abuela's garden.

Teaching Paco how to play guitar.

I know you were loved. Who loved you?

She held his hand and her mind erupted with a thousand butterflies. Flying dreams were her favorite, and he was the only one who had flying dreams. They soared over the world, perched on the shoulder of Christ the Redeemer overlooking Rio. She played fútbol with him and his cousins in the forgotten streets of Puerto Viejo. She planted tomato vines with his abuela in Barcelona. She danced at his sister's quinceañera.

She was no longer haggard and wistful. She was gleefully optimistic. The dead had imparted their last wish of life to her, entrusting her with all their unrequited hopes.

She asked the pathologist a thousand questions.

"Does the mind stop when our heart stops or does it go on dreaming?"

"The mind stops when it can get no oxygen."

"But could it live on? Could it still dream?"

"No. When the heart stops, the mind stops. With no mind, you cannot dream."

"But, can their souls dream?"

"What is a soul? You think it so simple, to measure a human soul?

To weigh it on our scales like the stomach, liver and lungs?"

"I think souls can dream," Flora told him.

One day, she heard a name curl around Javier's mind, so clear and powerful it was as if he had spoken it: Antonio. Antonio. She envisioned the dark-haired, energetic boy in the apple orchard.

"Flora! This is the second time you've been sleeping at the desk." The pathologist was furious.

"No, I wasn't sleeping. I was—"

"The family of Javier Ortiz is here to claim the body."

"The family? Finally?"

"They had to travel from California."

Her heart sank a little, because they were from California and not Rio or Barcelona or Puerto Viejo or someplace she and Javier had explored together.

"I need you to get the paperwork in order. Unless you're going to fall asleep again."

Javier's family were cold and indifferent. The mother's face seemed to be a thousand years old, like overly stressed whitewashed leather. The father was short, stout, and his face had chiseled forgotten sharp edges. They both glared at Flora. They refused to cry. A small, dark-haired boy hid behind the mother's legs. Flora did not think it was appropriate to let someone so young know of the dead. The mother turned her back to Javier.

"He's broken my heart a thousand times. I warned him this would happen. His life would come to no good," she told the pathologist. "There are no tears left."

Flora approached them cautiously. "Which one of you is Antonio?"

They bristled. "There is no Antonio in our family."

"Not a cousin or ..."

The pathologist shushed her. The body would be cremated and they would sprinkle the ashes.

"Are you going to sprinkle them in an apple orchard? Or a garden?"

They bristled. "Who is this? Why do you speak of our Javier? What do you know of him?

"She's just a resident. She's just learning." The pathologist apologized.

"Have her learn from someone else's family."

After they left, the pathologist was all too happy to announce Flora's rotation was over. He assured her this would be her last day in pathology.

"Do you think that's what people want in a doctor? Someone who sleeps all the time, acting like their head is in the clouds? Not even the dead want that kind of doctor," he said

Her last job was to complete paperwork on Javier, so the body could be moved. Alone in the morgue, she went to cold storage, grabbed the handle on Javier's berth and slowly pulled out the body to take one last look. She wept. Such a beautiful man with dreams of butterflies and apple orchards. Such a treasure to be turned to dust.

"One last dream mi vida," he whispered to him. "One last dream."

She put her arms around him and lifted him until his head rested lifelessly against her shoulder, pressed into her. She looked to heaven, like the Madonna in the Pieta. She closed her eyes. A scent of apples flooded the room.

Author's Bio:

Dawn DeAnna Wilson is the author of two novels, *Saint Jude* and *Leaving the Comfort Café. Saint Jude* explores the issues associated with bipolar disorder and was listed in "The Big Book of Teen Reading Lists: 100 Great, Ready-to-Use Book Lists for Educators,

Librarians, Parents, and Teens" by Nancy Keane. Her play, *Jesu of Fondue*, has been produced by community and regional theatre groups. Her work has appeared in publications such as *Writer's Digest, Byline, The Lutheran Journal* and *Dr. Hurley's Snake Oil Cure.* She resides in Wilmington, NC. (www.dawndeannawilson.com)

Hada

By Magaly Garcia

"Don't leave the house.
Don't make a sound if someone knocks.
Don't open the door to strangers.
Don't answer the phone unless it's
my number on caller id,
but if you have an emergency,
call me.

Don't open the curtains.
Don't peek out the windows.
Don't turn on the stove.
Don't keep the fridge door open.
Don't eat junk food after seven.
Don't leave dishes unwashed.
Don't watch TV on high volume.
Don't turn on the porch light until after dark.

Do you understand, m'ija?"

"Yes, mami."

"I'll try to be back from work by ten."

"Okay, mami."

⌘

Laughing,
Paloma steps outside in a thunderstorm,
dances
beneath
pat-patting-patternless
raindrops
until she halts
mid-twirl for a teeny, spherical cerulean glow
hovering by her soaked mailbox,
within Mami's dead Corona de Cristo's thorns.

Pause. A breath, a blink—

"Firefly? Those don't burn blue.
Cucuy? Those aren't real.

Right?"

—white lightning cracks the sky
rebounds on earth,

Paloma scrambles
back to her house,
slams the screen door
behind her.

⌘

A creak from the front door
startles Paloma
    up from her pillow,

Mami's home.

Instead of leaving the bed to hug Mami,
Paloma sees
bright blue
    illuminating her feet—a light pulsing
within her room's black,
    shaded strewn-about toys,
gold-spine fairytale books,
    in its nightlight
    heartbeat.

    Pause. A breath, a blink—

"What's your name? Mine's Paloma.
You're very pretty. Want to play with me?"

    —it dances over her sheets,
    floats towards her round face.

    Closer it flies:
a humanesque form
about an inch tall,
abdomen

emitting fluorescent glimmer,
barely-engraved-face
like mall mannequins,
no fingers or toes,
translucent skin,
dragonfly
wings protruding from its back—

Paloma strokes one wing.

It flutters away, dives down,
covers its glow
with the bed skirt,
not to come out
until
the following night,
again on overmorrow's nightfall.

⌘

Unfamiliar—Criatura—Desconocida
invisible to everyone but Paloma.

She wishes
she could ask the creature
what it is,
but it does not speak, only twinkles.

She checks out books
from school, looks at illustrations:

Tinker Bell's wings and tiny figure.

"Are you a fairy?"

She points to the book's image.

The creature's beams explode,
sparkle brighter
than before.

⌘

They play
in night's obscurity for years
until
Mami stomps in one midnight:

"You are not five anymore!
You're in high school
and have exams tomorrow!
Quit your make-believe friend!
Go to sleep!"

Pause. A breath, a blink—

"Perdón, mami."

—Paloma and the hada turn from each other.

They sink:
one underneath magical princess sheets,

the other to the bed's bottom.

⌘

For one month
Paloma tries talking
    to classmates,
meeting conversational dead-ends,
    encountering snarky looks
upon mentioning fantasy books, miniature toys,
    wishing for sightings
of giggling flickers
and airborne bouncing.

Summer begins.
Paloma whispers into the dark:

"Do you want to know
my *exam scores?"*

The orb zips out
from the gap between floor
and
closet door,
zooming towards the
bed's head, brightening the room
with shiny, buzzy wings.

⌘

It is her newborn nephew's celebration.

Mami is hosting
the fiesta.

Tíos and neighbors spread out in the small yard,
tías and women invade the kitchen,
children and teens cluster
in the living room
for card games,
for VHS cartoons.

Stuck in too tight jean skirt, secondhand sneakers,
sweaty sweater and curls
gelled back
in a face-pulling ponytail,
Paloma counts minutes with a bat
fisted in her 14-year-old palms.

Alone in her room she sits,
watching her uncles
hoist up the piñata with a thick cord:

the short one with Vicente Fernandez's moustache
skids on his rusty Toyota roof,
the tall one with Ricky Martin's shake-your-bon-bon hips
slips on the roof tiles above her room.

Paloma does not hear her bedroom door open.

She does not see

her primo saunter in,
she does feel
her mattress dip low.

She turns around,
squints at her cousin.

"What?"

"Why are you here all alone?"

"I'm waiting."

"For the piñata?"

"Sí."

"Me too."

Silence envelops them,
save the men's grunting
outside.

Her cousin's hand stretches
across Paloma's back,
slides up
to her bra strap.

Pause. A breath, a blink—

Paloma recoils.

She raises the bat
over her shoulder.
Paloma sees
the rainbow seven-horned piñata

instead of her primo's pubescent-hairy face

—the hada swoops up from an open drawer,
yanks back his finger—

the bone's crack
snaps the previous silence,

now drowned by the primo's doggish howl,
by Paloma's high weepy laugh
the hada can't pry her fingers from the bat!

Her primo's mother speeds in
slaps Paloma's crown,
like a drum roll, screams:

"You dress too sexy!
You overreacted!
He was only playing!
He was only playing!"

—and before the hada zooms to fracture more fingers,

Mami enters the room too,

snags the bat from Paloma's hands,

swings at the primo, at his mother,
hunts them down
throughout the house,
bashing food,

splitting glass plates,
the screen door,
and maybe an arm, definitely bruising skulls.

The tíos and men guffaw,
hold all three apart,
take the bat from Mami,
drag the primo and his mother
away.

The tías and women
glare at Paloma,
at Mami,
follow the primo and his mother
out the torn screen door.

⌘

When left
in earsplitting nothingness,
standing on tattered emptiness,

Mami drives open-armed into Paloma,
apologizing,
apologizing,
apologizing,
as Paloma
forgives,
forgives,
forgives,

as the hada,
sitting on bat-squished Mexican chocoflan,
watches,
watches,
watches

Paloma and Mami

clean the house,
rip open the abandoned piñata,
feast on chamoy-flavored candies,
sleep in Mami's room
beside a pile of
marzipan wrappers.

Author's Bio:
Magaly Garcia received an MFA in Writing & Publishing from Vermont College of Fine Arts. She has been published in Along the River III, University of Texas Rio Grande Valley's The Gallery (2013, 2015), VCFA's Synezoma, Francis House (2017), The Chachalaca Review (2018), and Boundless 2018: Rio Grande Valley International Poetry Festival. She lives in south-south Texas, is currently working on a YA hybrid thing, and when not writing she is summoning fantasmas to haunt her cat and cacti.

Where Dead Men are Buried

By Susan Breall

Dead men are buried under my grandfather's farm. We found this out by accident one summer many years ago, when my brother Jonah and I were sent away to live with our grandparents in Sebastopol. I had just finished fifth grade at Roosevelt Elementary School and Jonah had just finished third. It was our father who insisted we spend the summer on the farm, while he tended to our mother during her cancer treatments. At first, our mother was against the idea, but later she relented and took us both down to the bus station herself. She cried in front of every passenger as we boarded the large blue and white bus. The ride out to the country was tedious. So full of jerks, twists and braking, during the six hour journey, Jonah threw up three separate times into a large plastic produce bag, before we reached our final destination.

As boys unfamiliar with the ways of the country, it took several weeks to adapt, once we arrived. We had never visited the farm before, nor had we visited much with our grandparents themselves, except on the rare occasion when they came to our house in the city for a special celebration or a funeral. We soon learned not to bother our grandfather, when he went out to survey his acreage and plant walnut trees. We also learned to stay out of our grandmother's way, when she brined the cucumbers we picked from the vegetable garden, or when she boiled large pots of raspberries, which she gathered with over-sized gloves from the tangle of bushes by the drying shed. It took weeks to realize, however, that Grandma wanted us out of the kitchen all the time, whether she was cooking, brining, baking or not. She had a dislike for dirt and a similar dislike for boys who tracked dirt into her house.

It also took time for us to get used to the idea that spiders lived in the bottom corners of the drying shed and in the garage rafters. The shed was little more than a broken down old structure with a tin roof and wooden shelves containing abandoned jars of nails, car lubricants, tools and mechanical parts. Jonah refused to enter after he fell asleep one hot afternoon on a moldy recliner near its back entrance, only to wake to a cellar spider crawling along his ankle.

We eventually got used to almost everything about the farm, even the growling German shepherd called Frank, who wandered now and then onto the property from the adjacent cherry orchard. The only thing we never got used to was the wind in the night when we were alone in our bedroom. Whenever the wind kicked up and shook the large Juneberry bushes, growing against the bedroom window, we heard a scraping noise the branches made as they rubbed up against the pane. This noise sounded as if someone was trying to get into our bedroom. It kept us awake and frightened us, although I pretended to not be afraid.

After a few weeks, Jonah began to wake up in the middle of the night, believing the caretaker of the farm was standing outside the window trying to get into our room to attack us. The caretaker was an old Chinese man named Fung Hoy. He lived in a small house on the back side of the property. Mr. Hoy's skin was brown and weathered from his years of disking the orchard. His face was creased like wet cotton shirts hung out to dry before ironing. Jonah and I estimated him to be about a thousand years old, but his body was strong and capable of digging up large mounds of dirt for planting.

During the day, we sometimes ran into him when we were in the orchard, searching for agates or pieces of obsidian. We found rose quartz, salt crystals, and if we were lucky, unbroken arrow heads hidden in the dirt. Once in a while, we even found pieces of old dinner plates and grinding stones, buried from long ago. During our rock hunts, Mr. Hoy was either on the tractor planting trees or feeding the chickens. When he looked our way, we would shout out made up words in a fake tonal language and run in the opposite direction toward the back of the orchard. We were wild, rude and unafraid of him in the daylight, but In the middle of the night, we hid under our covers and refused to open the window curtains to see if he might be standing outside.

The afternoons dragged on with a relentless tedium of a slow drip faucet. There were few books in the house. Sometimes we would walk down the road about a mile to the Sebastopol High School and swim in the outdoor pool or walk over to the public library. If we were lucky, our grandfather would drive us to the library in his old green pick – up, which had more rust than paint. Or, he'd drive us out to Gibby's Corner Store, about three miles away to buy Batman comic books and magazines, while he stopped at the bank on business.

One particularly windy night, I was reading a Mad Magazine with a flashlight when Jonah woke up with a scream. I calmed him down and told him to go back to sleep. He refused, insisting Mr. Hoy was standing just outside the window. After a great deal of discussion and trepidation, I mustered up the courage to pull back my father's childhood window curtains, printed with images of gun slinging cowboys and arrow wielding Indians and shine my flashlight. We saw no one standing outside the window or hiding in the bushes. After further fervent discussion, we decided to sneak over to the caretaker, Mr. Hoy's house. We wanted to peer through his kitchen window and see if he was home.

We put on our shoes and slipped out the back as quietly as we could. There was barely the snap of the outer screen door as it sprung shut behind us. We left our grandparents sleeping and ran across the wet grass and jumped over our cardboard fort. We passed trays of prunes left out to air dry on wooden slats near the barn. That's when we heard a long strange howl of wind come across the orchard as we neared the old caretaker's house. The wind swept through the trees and caused a tarp to fly off a tractor and tumble sideways into the dirt.

Mr. Hoy had been living in that house for many years, yet we all referred to the house as the old *caretaker's* house, never Mr. Hoy's place. Jonah and I knew little about him, other than the fact he spoke broken English and helped out on the farm. While we ran to check on him, I realized I had no idea if Mr. Hoy lived alone, with a family, or whether he had a pet rabbit or even a pet turtle.

A dim light in the kitchen could be seen. We crouched down and peered inside the grimy cobwebbed window. We could make out Mr. Hoy moving about in the back of the kitchen. I watched him place a large ripe orange inside a red and gold-leafed side - less wooden structure, which looked like a box-kite or a small house without walls. Inside this structure, next to the orange, was a small framed photograph of a woman. Who was she? The scent of incense, burning from a brass bowl on the sink, wafted from the partially open window. We saw him walk to the Formica table, take another orange out of a brown paper bag and place it in the same wooden structure beside the first one. Then we watched him bow three times in the direction of the oranges and the photograph. When he was done bowing, he turned his body in the opposite direction and began to bow all over again. After bowing in all four directions, he sat down cross legged on the wooden floor and began to chant.

At first Mr. Hoy's chanting sounded like the barking of an

elephant seal I once saw on a National Geographic television special. Jonah began to giggle. I quickly motioned for him to keep quiet. As we listened closely, the chanting turned into a low and long, somber wail. In this wail, I heard the wind moving across the orchard. I heard the sound of the Juneberry bushes brush up against a window. I heard the hard cry of the lost and tired men who might never find their way home.

I remained transfixed, until Jonah suddenly gasped and made a jerky movement away from a crawling spider on the window sill, one he could make out from the light within. Mr. Hoy stopped chanting and quickly got up off the floor. He went to the sink and grabbed a meat cleaver. We both jumped up and ran back through the orchard the way we came, never stopping to see if he was chasing us. Breathless and afraid, we somehow managed to get to the back screen door, and into our bedroom without waking anyone up. We avoided Mr. Hoy after that night.

It was three weeks later that we actually encountered him face to face. Unusual summer rains had soaked the cherry and plum trees for days. Mr. Hoy and our grandfather went out planting trees in the back of the property as soon as those rains let up. Jonah and I waited every day until late afternoon, when they were finally done planting. That's when we went to the freshly upturned soil searching for arrowheads.

On a particularly hot day, after we started our afternoon dig, my shovel unearthed something remarkable: a human skull. Awestruck, I picked up the skull for closer inspection and tried to blow away particles of surface dirt from the top part of the cranium. I could see teeth still lodged in the lower part of the jaw. We stood there examining this extraordinary find when Mr. Hoy walked up to us. As soon as I saw him, I let the skull drop back into the hole. In his best English, Mr. Hoy told us return to the house and bring our Grandfather out.

We ran all the way, yelling about a dead man in the orchard.

When our grandfather emerged, we explained we hadn't actually seen a dead man, but we'd found a skull. As we walked, Jonah added — Mr. Hoy may have killed this man with his cleaver. Our grandfather walked us back to the spot where Mr. Hoy stood, waiting. Both men conversed, set the skull aside and then started shoveling dirt away from the ever deepening hole. They found several large teeth and what looked like a leg bone. Our grandfather calmly walked back to the house and called Sheriff Ahern.

The sheriff arrived about a half hour later, along with another man and a woman. The man was the medical examiner and woman was an archeologist from a nearby state university. After taking them out to the dig, our grandfather went back to the house to wait for all three to finish examining the site. Jonah and I stood around the grove and watched. We were told to stand back, while various preliminary tests were conducted on the teeth, the bones, and samples of the dirt. These tests seemed labor intensive. The sheriff wanted the tests done immediately before the dig could be compromised in any way by wind, rain, or human meddling. Later, they would take the objects back to the lab for further analysis. I looked around for Mr. Hoy, but didn't see him. Once the tests were completed, the sheriff and his crew walked back with us to the farm house.

Sheriff Ahern told my grandfather the preliminary results revealed a man and a bear had been buried side by side in the orchard. Confirmatory tests needed to be performed. The man most probably belonged to the Miwok tribe, so the tribal elders needed to be consulted. More than likely the entire orchard had once been an Indian burial mound. The sheriff had marked the area surrounding the hole with yellow hazard tape. He planned to return, after the confirmatory tests, with members of the Miwok tribal council.

We learned the bones were hundreds of years old. Two tribal elders were on their way over to the farm to perform a burial ceremony for the remains. Jonah and I were ecstatic at the prospect of watching an Indian ceremony. We envisioned Indians coming on the property dressed in full regalia with head dress and tomahawks, like the Indians depicted on the curtains of our father's childhood bedroom windows.

When the tribal elders arrived with Sheriff Ahern, we were extremely disappointed. One man wore a red plaid shirt, the other a shirt made out of plain blue denim. Both wore jeans and tennis shoes. Other than their pony tails and brown skin, there was nothing about these men to indicate they came from the Miwok tribe, or any other tribe for that matter. We walked quietly with them out to the hole where I found the skull. Even our grandmother came along, willing to brave the dirt field in order to watch the ceremony take place.

Soon the Native men circled the hole. Their circling became a rhythmic dance and chant. Through their chanting, I imagined the rustling of the Juneberry bushes. In their chant, I could almost hear the mournful cry of the wind sweep through the trees. The old dog started barking. I looked back and noticed Mr. Hoy standing off in the distance, amid broken pieces of flint and rock, in the midst of old growth walnut trees and freshly turned earth from new saplings. Although he stood alone and apart, it seemed he was listening to that same broken wind.

Author's Bio:

Susan M. Breall's short stories appear in the 2018 anthology Impermanent Facts, the 2019 anthology of Dreamers Writing, and Paragon Press' 2018 Martian Chronicle. She was a finalist in the 2017 Retreat West short story competition as well as the Firedrake Books short story competition. Her stories have been published in Thewritelaunch.com, Jewishfiction.com, and Twosisterswriting.com. By day she presides over cases involving abused, abandoned or neglected children. By night she writes short stories.

Under the Eye of the Crow

By VT Dorchester

It was a late mid-September afternoon in eastern Montana territory. Here, the Great Plains started dying. They began their rolling towards the mountains, increasingly pockmarked by gatherings of trees. An outlaw by the name of Garreth Weeks stopped alongside such a thicket. He checked his horse's tender foreleg. He thought of the sweet crunch of an apple. He looked up. He looked down the barrels of three guns.

Were he entirely sober and well, the men never would have surprised him. As it was, the familiar warning, a coolness to everything he touched and the tenderness in his fingertips, told him he had a fever rising. It was over two years since the doctors had condemned him to slow death by consumption. He and fever were old friends.

Now the men vanished over a hill with his horse, gun, and his summer earnings. They had taken his coat, hat, blanket, water and whiskey. They had taken his shirt, waistcoat and undershirt. He cursed the men and his carelessness. He reckoned he was twenty-five miles from shelter, and was almost completely naked. At least he still had his boots and drawers. Not even while outnumbering him three to one did those men choose to tangle with the look that came into his eye at the suggestion he take his drawers off. Two of the robbers had red hair; the third man was brown-haired and darker. All were taller than him and were riding duns. He would track them down. He could not afford to let them go. For now he was the one in trouble.

A crow, flying high, twisted its neck and brought a bright eye around to watch what happened below. Weeks had been following an old trail, little used. Now that the robbers were gone, he could see no one, and thought himself alone. Early that morning, he had seen a small traveling family of Absaroka Indians riding through the grasses far off the trail. He had no particular fear of the Absaroka and they had made no sign of interest in him, and so he forgot them. He counted on no help, until he reached the main road and no drink, unless it rained. He walked three hours before sundown, slapping at whining mosquitoes. He realized with a pang that with his coat, the bandits had taken his tintype of Anna. This was the thing that was the most precious of all things. The darkness of a new moon meant he had to stop or risk losing the way. There were ways to build a fire without matches, but he was a man of towns and cities and did not know them. He thought he smelled smoke, but saw nothing.

Those three men would regret crossing him, as other men had regretted crossing him before. He had broken at least six of the commandments, debated if he had broken the sixth commandment or not. He was a veteran. He was a sometimes thief, a brawler. He had robbed people, but he had never left them this vulnerable, with no water, fire or shelter.

The night sweats came. Once, on the brink of sleep, he thought he heard footsteps, and lurched upright. All he saw were stars. All he smelled was dust and grass. All he heard was his own breathing. Eventually, near morning, he did sleep and mercifully, he had escaped visitation from his nightmares. Weeks woke to a scratchy throat, cough, thirst and a familiar pain in his chest. He walked the trail. He didn't dare take off his boots to see what was becoming of his feet. The boots were not built for walking, and neither was he. His feet ached and burned at the ankles. Twice he turned to stare behind him, but there was no one there, only memories.

Around noon, he stumbled over a rock and fell. He remembered watching dolphins crossing the sea to America. His nose was bleeding. The sun felt good, warming his febrile body. He wanted to stay and rest. *More than four thousand miles from the place I was born, I might die.* The crow lazily circled from on high. It watched. Weeks thought of punishments for those who had stolen from him and got up again. His skin prickled with sun burn. His tongue was leaden. Mosquitoes latched to him and now he was too tired to keep flicking them away. He let them feed. At a place where a prairie dog colony had mown the grass near bare, he stopped to vomit. Prairie dogs squeaked their alarm.

If it were only a little later in the year, there would be frost on the ground. "For small mercies, let thee be grateful," Garreth Weeks said to the dogs, and they dashed to their holes. The lessons of his stern American parents and their Bible returned in pieces at odd moments. He had not been inside a church or attended a service for years. Not since the horror of Ebenezer Creek in Georgia. Weeks slowly made his way, slowly shrinking for want of water and skin slowly burning for want of shelter. He hummed *Shall We Gather by the River* for want of company.

The horizon was beginning to pulsate. It bruised and swirled and gathered cold clouds. Garreth Weeks tried to keep his eyes on the ground ahead of him, to avoid the shapes taking form above. The sky-bruise was darkening. It took on the same color as the Ebenezer did in his mind. He despaired of what might soon manifest. He stumbled again and again. Cramps speared through his legs. He heard laughter. A wind began, coming down from the north. Snow wind.

Clenching his fists, he spoke with the dead.

"I tried to help you," Weeks cried out. "I did try. Please believe me." It was true, but the water of Ebenezer Creek had been too swift and deep. He could no more swim it than the dead could. The Southern cavalry had grown closer and the orders were to move on. He left them, after watching the bridge he had crossed safely be drawn away. He left the frantic women and children and old men, to drown or return to their enslavement. So few had managed to cross on their own. He was only a soldier. Only following orders.

"Forgive me," he muttered inside his throbbing skull.

Another crow flew low above him. He lost his sense of time and distance. His hands were so cold, yet his thirst was a cedar blaze in his throat.

If I get out of this alive, I swear, I will do nothing that isn't for Anna. I know I promised before. She is the only family I have. The only promise I have left. I will see that Anna will be cared for before I die.

Then Garreth Weeks didn't feel his thirst anymore, nor the pain in his chest, or his bleeding feet. He could see himself, from the outside. He floated above himself like the crow. He watched as a desperate man clung to life, a man in his thirties walking across dry prairie in front of a storm. The sky was slowly changing from purple to pink, a soft gentle glow. It grew around his wandering body. He could see small grains of grass rubbing together at the tops of the drying stalks that grew alongside the path. They were each—beautiful and miraculous. Weeks didn't hurt anymore. He stood still and closed his eyes in great relief.

Am I dying?

He could no longer feel his feet, his hands nor body.

But Anna…

And damnation. I cannot hope to escape damnation. This is a trick. I am not ready. I am not going.

I am doomed, but Anna is innocent. Let me help her.

Please.

Someone spoke his name.

Four miles from the next town, he could take himself no further. Weeks fell. The Absaroka who had taken to the trail behind him now came close. They whispered to each other about what they should do. One splashed a few drops of water on the man's forehead.

Garreth Weeks opened his eyes and then sank into that bruised darkness.

Author's Bio:

V.T. Dorchester is the fringed-buckskin-wearing alter ego of a plains-city-raised writer. They now live in small-town interior British Columbia, Canada. Most of what they misunderstand and love about the American 'Wild West' they attribute to the great 'classic' Hollywood westerns. This publication is the second public appearance of the character Gar Weeks, who also lives in an as yet unpublished novella. V.T. believes westerns do not only have to be written by, for, or about old white guys, although those stories can be cool. They admit the closest thing to a horse they have is a poodle.

From Trina to *T*

By Susan Breall

When I was twelve years old, I met an old lady who sold magic wands on the corner of Ivy and Market Street. I have no idea how old she was, though she seemed ancient back then. Her wands were long thin tree branches. They were spindly like the old lady's arms. I spent the previous week searching the Internet for magic wands. Most of the magic wand sites sold nothing more than plastic, fake, fairy sticks with sparkling glitter stars on their ends. I wasn't looking for a toy. I was looking for real magic.

I found the old lady standing a block down from her usual spot. She had brown skin like my own. When I walked up to her and asked the price of a wand, she stared at my braided hair before answering. I reached up and felt the ends of my hair to see if they were out of place.

"It all depends child — on what you might be needin' one for." She spoke like she was from Jamaica. Other than her accent, she seemed ordinary. She could have been my great aunt or my great aunt's cousin. She continued to stare like she saw me from the inside out. I noticed her eyes were the color of dark green olives.

"Without tellin' me why you want one, I won't be able to help you."

"I'm not sure you can help me, even if I do tell you."

"Well then, you won't be needin' anything from me. These are special, you know."

How could I share the truth about the boy who had pushed me up against the wall in the school stairwell the week before? How could I explain his hot breath in my face or the cold wet of unforgiving concrete at my back, trapped in the corner with my head banging the wall, the echo of footsteps never reaching the top landing? How could I tell her all he said and did, or explain that I needed the magic to protect myself? I hadn't told a soul. I didn't want to start with her.

"A mean nasty boy ran up behind me last week and grabbed my journal right out of my hands. He grabbed my arm and tore a hole in my sweater."

"You should report him."

"I can't snitch. I just need to put a bad luck curse on him, or a good luck spell on me."

"How do you know these branches are magic?"

"I saw you light one on fire and wave it over your head when I came out of the YWCA last Saturday. When the cops got there, I went across the street for a candy bar and this guy behind the counter told me you knew magic."

"Listen to me. What you saw was a warning. I was sendin' a message to a man I wanted out of the neighborhood, a man I needed to threaten. In this neighborhood, we have a whole different way of communicatin' with each other, whether it's by hangin' a pair of shoes over a telephone wire or settin' fire to a tree branch, you don't need any tree branches to scare that boy of yours you think so mean-nasty. He did nothin' real bad that I can see."

At that moment, I knew I had to tell her what the boy actually did if there was any chance of her helping me. I was convinced that this old brown lady knew enough magic and curses to go after him and protect me. I let out a heavy hearted sob and took my time explaining. When I was done, she made room for me on the stair next to her. It took several minutes to compose myself.

"Normally, I wouldn't go putin' myself out for the likes of a girl I know nothin' about. Under normal conditions, I would tell you to fly away. But this very same thing happened to me. I don't know your name girl, but I know you."

She wanted this boy's full name and address. I spelled them out. Then she pointed down the street to two men who were half hidden in a doorway. These men had been standing at the end of the block the entire time we spoke.

"Those young men are my nephews. You will find them to be extremely helpful in situations like these. They speak the language of the street. They know how to sniff out evil and set things right. Tell me the name of your school." I not only told her the name of my school, I gave her the exact address.

"Now, off with you. I'll take care of things." As I walked away, the men kept their eyes on me, until I disappeared around the corner.

I realized that day that there are different forms of magic. There is magic in feeling protected from all that is bad with the world. There is magic in the beauty of walking down a street unafraid. There is magic in the way sunlight filters through the leaves of tree branches swaying in the park on a rainy day. I went back to my grandmother's house and stayed inside for the remainder of the afternoon. I convinced my grandmother I was sick and she kept me home for a week.

When I finally returned, the boy was not in class. I stopped seeing him in the hallways. He didn't come to homeroom or algebra. I peaked in the lunch room and noticed he wasn't there. I was fairly certain the old lady and her nephews had gotten rid of the boy, but I still avoided the stairwell and the back doors of the building. I never walked alone into an empty room. Later, I was told by another student that something scared the boy so badly his mother arranged for a transfer to another school. We were never officially told the reason he left. He just seemed to have disappeared—like magic.

After his disappearance, I was able to finish the rest of middle school without a hitch. That summer, I lied about my age, said I was sixteen, and got a job at a burger joint called *The Mighty Bite* bussing tables. I began reading everything I could find in the library about power, what it was and how to acquire it. I learned power was a pathway to freedom. Freedom was the ultimate power, the ability to go anywhere unencumbered, to be in full swing. One book defined power as knowing someone else's secrets. I had plenty of my own.

I also came to recognize the important role certain people of affluence could play in my life. Making powerful connections was key, like having a loaded gun in my hip pocket. I decided to go back and visit the old lady and her magic wands. I showed up every Friday afternoon with strawberry milk shakes and burgers from work. We sat on the stoop of one of the apartment buildings, ate and discussed the comings and goings on the street. I often sat with my shoes off and warmed my feet on the sunbaked sidewalk. Neighbors walked over to our side of the street to trade used clothes, stolen electronics, and gossip. The street, where we sat, was a small part of a large district of a much larger town, but it became my entire world, a part of me, as familiar as my own worn out jeans.

The old lady, her nephews, and the rest of the people on that street gave me a new name. Instead of Trina, they called me "T." And in a way, they became my family. They taught me the significance of a window shade pulled half way down, and what it meant to throw sneakers over a telephone wire. I was taught the precise way to set fire to a tree branch. I was shown where to hide the nephews' stolen cell phones when the cops appeared. I learned a whole different way of 'communicatin'. Street language became a fluent dialect for me.

What I learned most of all that summer was, the old lady with her olive green eyes had been right. She knew me. I was just like her and I hadn't even known it. What happened in that stairwell so many months ago, was just the beginning of my transformation. That summer, I emerged from the chrysalis stage I learned about in science class. I came out of those shadowy stairwells, where I once had been cornered, and spoke up, even broke the rules. I learned to love the way freedom felt.

Author's Bio:

Susan M. Breall's short stories appear in the 2018 anthology Impermanent Facts, the 2019 anthology of Dreamers Writing, and Paragon Press' 2018 Martian Chronicle. She was a finalist in the 2017 Retreat West short story competition as well as the Firedrake Books short story competition. Her stories have been published in Thewritelaunch.com, Jewishfiction.com, and Twosisterswriting.com. By day she presides over cases involving abused, abandoned or neglected children. By night she writes short stories.

Madam Ursa's Performing Bears

By Robert Allen Lupton

Nothing looked like a circus all dressed up for Friday night. In the evening, the midway, with its game booths, exhibitions and most importantly the Big Top, was as brightly lit and vibrant in color as the neon strip in Las Vegas. Women were beautiful; men were handsome and strong. The animals were happy and well groomed.

The circus would come into town and overnight, it transformed a vacant field, a feed lot, or a dirt parking lot, outside a high school football stadium, into a magical place where the locals could forget their cares and woes from everyday life and bask in the harsh glare of multicolored neon lights.. The three ring Big Top attracts families, and games of chance beckoned the reckless and unwary. AThe sideshow was filled with attractions and freaks, real and pretend. Children gaped in amazement at midgets, stilt men, and bearded ladies.

This Camelot of amazement only stayed in town for two or three nights.

If it stayed any longer, the locals might have looked too closely at the man behind the curtain. People might have noticed the torn and patched canvas or banners, so glorious under the nighttime lights, tattered. . The beautiful men and pretty women were are exhausted grimand travel worn under the harsh noon day sun. On close examination, their costumes didn't fit as well in the daylight either. They'd been taken in or let out to fit many people as they'd been handed down from one performer to another over the years. Without their makeup, clowns were hollow eyed, haggard, and appeared old.

The circus wasn't quite as grand, once you'd seen the backstage. Without bangles, beads, sequins, or knee high boots, the people were just people in sweaty shirts and dirty shoes. They spent their days pretty much the same way as farmers and ranchers did in town. They had to pay their bills, feed the animals, cook their food, and mend their clothes. They had to clean up after the animals the same as a rancher did his. Circus folk didn't shovel cow flop or horse manure, they dealt in more exotic excrements.

The ringmaster's wife, Katrina the Tattooed Lady, liked to say, "Everybody's job is to keep food on the table and the wolf away from the door." She didn't know quite what that really meant, but it fit in with a world view that thirty years of playing small towns had given her. Once they took off their costumes, people were all the same: doctors, lawyers, bankers, rock stars, clowns, acrobats, tumblers, and hootchie cootchie girls. Even old tattooed ladies had to eat, sleep, and go to work.

After a great night, the lot was littered with cotton candy cones, peanut bags, paper cups, and popcorn boxes to clean up the next morning. Policing the lot was just another way to shovel your share too. Cleaning the lot wasn't too bad on the good days, but picking up soggy popcorn and rain drenched cardboard, was endless. While the roustabouts cleaned the lot, the ringmaster was in his tent fighting the finances and dealing with the crap the local sheriff was handing out.

Sheriff Dan could spit tobacco as far as Katrina could. "Last night went just fine. I want your troop to behave the same way tonight and tomorrow night." He turned to the ringmaster. "Don't you be ripping off my folks the night you fold the tents. I expect the dancing girls to be dressed like Annette in all of those beach blanket bingo movies. You keep the midway games fair. No side bets between the carnies and my folks. Low stakes shell games and a little three card monte are alright. Teach our young men a good lesson, if the stakes don't get too high. I see one pickpocket, I'll shut you down in a minute." He continued, "I know we're all adults here, but you keep your men away from the local women. I want you to treat every woman in town like she's my own dear sister. Don't want your dancing girls pulling no badger games. Keep everything in the lights and keep everything fair. Do we understand each other?"

"Of course," said the ringmaster. "My folks want to put on a good show and spend some money while we're in town. I have tickets to tonight's show for you and your family. Be my guest in the ringmaster's box. How many tickets will you be needing?" He smiled.

'I'll take one for me and five for the mayor and his kids."

The ringmaster counted out the tickets and handed them along with five crisp one hundred dollar bills to the sheriff. The money was the unofficial licensing fee for the weekend. "Anything else I can do for you, sheriff?"

The sheriff took off his mirrored sunglasses and rubbed his ice blue eyes. He lowered voice out of Katerina's earshot. "I don't want your money, but I really admire that little lady who has those dancing bears. What's her name, Madame Ursa? I sure would like to meet her. Meet her and her bears, I mean."

The ringmaster looked into those cold blue eyes and lost his train of thought. "Yes, Madame Ursa. I'll let her know you want to meet her bears. How 'bout you meet me in front of the Big Top in an hour?"

"Can I bring something for her bears?"

"Sure. The bears are partial to scrambled eggs and bacon in the morning. They go through gallons of coffee most days. She feeds the bears the same things she feeds herself. I know they've had breakfast already, but a dozen donuts would be fine. They like donuts."

"OK." Sheriff Dan said. "I'll run into town and meet you in an hour. I'll bring donuts."

The sheriff enjoyed his power and he enjoyed the perks of his job. He loved women who couldn't say no. A few years ago, he only took advantage of women when the situation presented itself, but now he actively created opportunities. There was nothing better than a little lady that couldn't pay a parking ticket, although he had a special fondness for circus women in particular because he could manipulate them easiest.

Madame Ursa wasn't Adriana's real name. Adriana could have called herself Olga, Svetlana, Natasha, or Anastasia. Using any name for a Russian performer, other than those, would go right over everyone's head in heartland, USA. Adriana used the name *Ursa.* It was the Latin name for bear and, besides, it sounded vaguely Russian.

Her family had been circus performers for generations and she often played many roles during a performance. She worked with bears, spun on ropes, and sometimes she was even the human target in the knife throwing act.

She was young, single, attractive, and deflected countless advances from the locals. Unsolicited attention was a daily occurrence for circus women, attractive or not. Their exotic lifestyle and titillating costumes drew a bevy of lust struck suitors in every town. Some circus women took advantage of the local men. Led them on, let them buy gifts, promised them anything, but the women made sure they were on board when the circus left town. The old saying was: *All debts are paid when the wagons roll.*

Adriana had no interest in the occasional one night stand and she'd never found a man she cared about. She'd fallen for a magician a few years back, but his best trick had been to make himself disappear in Cairo, Illinois. After he vanished, Adriana decided that her mother was right. There were only two kinds of men – the ones who knew they were asses and the ones who didn't.

Occasionally she was asked to entertain a local *Lothario*, especially if he was a big fish in the local pond. When the mayor or sheriff came calling, she was polite and coy. She could always keep the men at bay. She cultivated an aura of dangerous mystery and feigned an inability to speak proper English. She wasn't averse to accepting gifts from time to time, but quid – pro - quo was out of the question. Not that she was a prude, she wasn't. But, She wanted a real relationship, and a pot-bellied southern sheriff with tobacco yellowed teeth and sweat stained clothing didn't make the cut. Men who blackmailed women angered her so.

The sheriff picked up two dozen donuts and met the ringmaster behind the Big Top. He radioed his office and told the dispatcher not to call him unless it was an emergency. "I'll be 10-20 at the circus for a while. I got a report of a 10-102: cruelty to animals, from one of the farmers who picked up a truck load of elephant crap this morning. He said something about the way the bears are being treated. I'm gonna meet with the bear lady and straighten her out."

The ringmaster led the sheriff to where "Ursa" and the bears were rehearsing. Marshall, the newest bear, was learning to juggle. The bear worked with brightly painted wooden balls about a foot in diameter. His paws were too big for anything smaller asand plastic or rubber balls couldn't survive teeth and claw.

Sheriff Dan made hungry eyed contact with Ursa. For a moment, she had a brief mental image of Snidely Whiplash twirling his moustache as he tied Little Nell's dad to the railroad track. His eyes were ice blue, and his body language told an old story.

The sheriff shook his head and said to the ringmaster, "Look at that. It's like the bear understands what she's saying. That's amazing. Introduce me to that little lady right now."

The ringmaster called Adriana over and introduced her as Ursa. Everyone used their performing names in public. It didn't matter who you were before you ran away to join the circus. You got a new name appropriate for your circus job. Even the ride and game operators had circus names for public use: *Ring toss Robert*, *Madame Fortuna,* and *Fingers* were self-explanatory.

"Ursa, I'd like you to meet Sheriff Forney, Dan Forney. I told him you'd be pleased to have him watch rehearsals and answer any of his questions."

"Howdy, Miss Ursa." The sheriff presented Ursa with two boxes of donuts like a pizza man making a delivery.

"Thank you." She clucked. "Oh, donuts! The boys do love donuts. It's nice to meet you, Sheriff Dan."

Ursa and the sheriff shook hands and the ringmaster excused himself, saying he needed to check on the rest of the performers. He raised his brow at Ursa. "Don't leave us all stuck in the donniker, Ursa. Your turn to keep things cool with the townie until we breakdown and move on. Sorry, but this is your horse to rope." Then he walked away, leaving the two with Ursa's bears.

Ursa understood the ringmaster. He basically told her not to leave the circus in the toilet. It was her job to keep the sheriff from closing the circus down, until the crew pulled up the stakes on the last day. If she kept the sheriff, or *fixer*, happy, he would keep the rest of the officials and townspeople in line. It was part of being in the circus. Ursa was fifth generation circus and was born knowing to be careful. Dealing with difficult men was like the "shell" game. Find the hidden pea under the walnut shell. A little distraction to fool the eye and the game was won. Most of the time, a difficult sheriff, mayor, or policeman was still dazzled by the glitz and glamour.

"Well sheriff, like to meet the boys? Come over to the practice ring. Bring those donuts, but let me feed them. Stay close, but don't get within reach. Remember the poem about the teeth that bite and the claws that snatch. They'll come for you in a heartbeat if they think you're a danger to them and they're very protective of me, so move slowly and don't upset them. They're skittish around strangers ," Sshe warned.

Ursa picked out a strawberry covered cake donut and held it up. "Trooper, Trooper," she called out. One of the bears stood on his back feet and lumbered clumsily toward Ursa. Trooper stopped six feet away from Ursa and sat down facing her. "Trooper, spin and dance. Spin and dance."

Trooper raised himself back up on his rear paws. He performed a credible step, ball, and change, followed with a box step, and then shuffled off to buffalo in a wide circle. He bowed and looked longingly at the strawberry donut.

"Trooper, don't bow, curtsy. You know people like it when you curtsy." She waved the donut in the air and said, "Show the sheriff a nice little curtsy."

The sheriff thought if any bear had angry eyes, it was Trooper. The bear stared daggers at Ursa, growled, and clumsily made an exaggerated curtsy. He fixed his green eyes on the donut and froze in attention.

"Good boy," said Ursa and she threw the donut to Trooper who swallowed without chewing. He dropped to all fours and lumbered away, when Ursa called another bear.

"Sarge, Sarge, front and center, Sarge." Sarge followed the movement of her right hand. He went right, left, or up and down when she moved her hand. When he was on his stomach, he rolled right and left at her gestures. He never took his amber eyes off Ursa's right hand as she put him through his routine. He received a vanilla crème donut for his trouble.

"Sheriff, this bear is named Marshall. He's a brown bear from up north. I rescued him in Michigan last season. He hasn't acclimated to the circus as well as the rest of my boys. He can't do any solo tricks yet, but he helps fill out the ring. Six bears is too many and four isn't enough. Isn't that right, Marshall? Now, Marshall, I know you want a donut. Do a somersault for the nice sheriff."

Marshall glared at them both and slowly bent and rolled over. It looked like the bear was doing a yoga move called the downward dog. Once in that position, Marshall ducked his head and walked his back feet forward until he tumbled over. The bear finished flat on his back with his arms and legs in the dead roach position. He flailed like an overturned turtle until he could flop to one side and lift himself to all fours.

"Madame Ursa, fascinating as this is, I really didn't come here to watch bear tricks." He huffed.

"Why sheriff. Don't you want to watch Chief juggle or Major play the accordion? I saved them for last. It's not fair if I don't let them do their little tricks and give them donuts."

"Give 'em the damn donuts. I don't care about their tricks. I'm here because, well…" He put himself in check, "because, I heard reports about animal abuse. Yeah, I heard that you mistreat these bears."

Madame Ursa smiled, "Now, sheriff, how could a little thing like me mistreat a bunch of great big bears? One of them could eat me right up."

The sheriff put a meaty hand on Ursa's smooth arm. "I have to follow up on all reports of animal abuse. I'm just doing my job. These animals look healthy enough, but I'll need to see where they live."

Ursa looked at him, curious.

"I want the ownership papers and medical records. In this state, all exotic animals need ownership papers and such. I want to be sure the bears are vaccinated for rabies, distemper, and things like that."

"I keep the records locked in my trailer. Let me finish working with my boys, feed them, and put them back in their cages. I'll show you my records afterwards."

"No hurry." The sheriff stroked her arm lightly. "How about I stop by your trailer after tonight's show and we can go over the records together. Would you like that?"

"Why, sheriff, I'd like that just fine." She touched his arm gently and purred, "That's a wonderful idea. Come by early and we'll walk the midway and then, I'll meet you after the show tonight. Reviewing paperwork is thirsty work. I'll chill a bottle of my family's wine to help us uncover everything you might want to see. Let's say about midnight, shall we?"

The sheriff hitched up his belt, and tipped his hat. "Midnight, then," he replied and walked away. There was something about the bears that bothered him, but he couldn't put his finger on it. It might be the way the bears did what they were told. It was like they understood her. "No, that can't be it," he thought to himself. "But, I guess if dogs can learn to follow commands, there's no reason bears couldn't."

He finally decided it was their eyes. The circus bears had differently colored eyes and none were black or brown eyed. He didn't think bears had green or amber eyes. It wasn't only the color of their eyes or the angry focus and attention he sensed, when they stared at him or Madame Ursa even. They looked sad. He dismissed his foolish notions. He didn't really care about the bears anyway. The only thing he truly cared about was, letting Madame Ursa convince him to ignore her non-existent paperwork. He looked forward to midnight. Suddenly,

Suddenly, his radio crackled and jarred him from his daydream. "Sheriff, we got a female shoplifter at the thrift store on Elm Street, can you take it?"

"10-4, I got it," replied the sheriff. He spent the rest of his day immersed in minor traffic violations, family disputes, and common petty issues found in every small town. Before he signed out for the day, he confirmed the evening's work assignments to ensure the circus traffic would flow smoothly. He didn't assign anyone to the circus lot, explaining he would personally be on site.

After the lot opened, the sheriff met Ursa and they walked the midway, listening to the talkers and barkers. He'd been on enough midways to understand how a talker would work the crowd until he gathered enough people outside his tent before 'turning the tip', meaning — move the crowd inside.

"Just one dollar gets you through the door to see seven, count 'em seven, of nature's special creatures." "The alligator man, the wolf woman, the poor lobster boy, the four legged woman, the wild man from Sumatra, and the mermaid twins are all inside this tent. These fish girls...the mermaids, left their oceanic home in Atlantis to tour the surface world and establish peaceful relations with us land people. Only people between eighteen and eighty allowed in the mermaid area. These girls don't wear clothes like we do. If you're under eighteen, you won't understand and if you're over eighty, you won't care."

The sheriff asked Ursa if any of the freaks were real.

"They're all real just like you and me, but some or more real than others. Some were born the way they are and some became what you see. The magic is that everyone sees what they want to see."

The sheriff listened to her explanation, although he wasn't convinced. He watched his townspeople line up to pay the entrance fee. He'd heard the spiel a hundred times before. Once inside, everyone would discover the mermaids were, twin sisters who didn't wear clothes like we did, but rather, they wore large fake seashells, strategically placed. They would be hanging with their heads and arms out of the water on the side of a large glass tank. Occasionally, one of them might swim around for a few seconds. The girls would answer questions about life in Atlantis and encourage the visitors to purchase eight by ten color glossy photographs, suitable for framing,, and autographed by both sisters. The intent of the sideshow was the same as the intent of the entire circus, GATM*: 'get all the money'*, words to live by in the circus. Not his problem. As long as no violence or robbery took place, the Sheriff Dan wasn't going to interfere. No need to upset the little lady walking the midway with him.

He lingered for a moment and watched the Three - card Monte dealer. He had nimble fingers and strong patter. Money the players lost, would be money well spent and a valuable lesson learned. Never bet against the man with cards. If he said the Jack of Spades would jump out of the deck, dance, and spit tobacco juice in your ear, you shouldn't take the bet. If you did, you'd have to get a handkerchief ready to dry your ear and say goodbye to your money. Young men had learned the hard way – a few dollars at a time.

Ursa rolled her eyes at the dealer upon eye contact. She then escorted the sheriff toward the rest of the booths, while she explained how the midway was set up. The best booth positions were the ones to the right. When people entered the circus through the gateway, most automatically walked to the right. So the strongest earners got booth space on that side. The booths to the left survived on whatever money the right side booths didn't take from country bumpkins, or "rubes," as they were called.

"I'll be darned," he said. "When I entered, I automatically went right!"

He watched the Big Top talker turn tip after tip at the show's entrance. "The best seats go first, ladies and gentlemen. You want that sweet little girl with you to see the clowns. Get her a seat up front. You want her to enjoy the show and remember the circus magic for the rest of her life." The patter never changed because it worked.

Madame Ursa excused herself to get ready for the show and the sheriff stepped to the front of the line where he used his free pass. He joined the mayor's family in the box seats. The mayor's kids were sticky with watered-down soft drinks, cotton candy, and popcorn and were pleading for corn dogs when the sheriff took his seat.

"You kids shut up. I'll buy corn dogs when the corndog man comes by." The mayor turned to the sheriff, "Art, I'm never comfortable with a circus. I hear all kinds of stories."

"Relax, I got this. You didn't hear any complaints last night. I met with the ringmaster and told him how things work in this town. No pickpockets, no short change artists, and no alibi booths." He glanced around then lowered his voice. "The women in the dancing shows have to keep their clothes on. I won't tolerate any key jobs or badger games. The worse that's is going to happen tonight is when one of our young guys loses twenty bucks because he can't find the Queen of Spades."

The mayor listened intently then asked, "What's a key job, I know what a badger game is."

Again, the sheriff kept his voice between them as the mayor's family busied themselves with the sights and sounds. "A key job is when a woman promises to meet a man after the show. She'll say she already has a room at a motel. 'Here's the key. I'll meet you tomorrow after the show. Will you pay for the room?' She gets him to pony up fifty dollars for the room. She probably has twenty keys. When twenty boys show up at the same room next night, the circus, and the girl will already be in Tuscaloosa."

The mayor was taken aback. "Are we really that stupid?"

"Our boys are like boys everywhere. Of course, they're that stupid. Anyway, none of that goes on in my town. You and your kids enjoy the show. The biggest problem you got is washing cotton candy out of their hair."

Curious again, the mayor asked, "What's an alibi booth?"

"It's a booth, uh....where you can't win no matter what. The booth operator always has a reason, an alibi, to explain why you didn't win: you leaned on the counter, you stood too close, or the prize fell over and you know you never hit it. There's always a reason to disqualify a winner. I won't allow that." The sheriff spoke in all seriousness.

The house lights dimmed and all attention went to the center of the arena as the ringleader took center stage.

"Ladies and gentlemen, parents, grandparents, and children of all ages, if I could have your attention, please. In just a few moments Odyssey Shows will present the greatest show on Earth, right here and right now under this very Big Top. Odyssey Shows has scoured the known and unknown world to present, for your enjoyment, the greatest, the handsomest, the most beautiful, and the most talented performers in the universe! They will perform amazing and unbelievable feats of skill and daring, as they risk their very lives for your viewing pleasure.

Rare and exotic animals have been sought out, captured, and trained for your enjoyment as well. You'll see lions and tigers and bears, oh my. Elephants! Arabian horses! And last, but not least, special dogs once trained to guard hidden temples in the Siamese jungles!"

The sheriff relaxed as the ringmaster requested the audience refrain from throwing anything at the performers. No flash photography was allowed. It was all part of the build up to make the show seem more dangerous than it was.

The mayor and his kids enjoyed the show from the opening parade to the grand finale.

Madame Ursa and her Russian Bears were a premier act. Boys danced, juggled, stood on their heads, and tossed a ball back and forth. One of the bears threw a plastic ball to another holding a plastic bat. Madame Ursa umpired. After a strike and a ball, the batter hit the plastic ball and lumbered around the ring while the other bears chased the ball. The running bear was out at the plate. He protested the call by crossing his arms and turning his back on the "umpire." He also kicked sawdust over home plate. When the cheers and applause died down, the bears gathered their props and paraded out behind Madame Ursa.

The sheriff was in such a hurry for the show to end, he hadn't noticed that Ursa never said a word to her bears during the show. The bears had moved seamlessly from trick to trick.

All he could think about was how good Madame Ursa looked in her tights and high heeled boots. By morning, he'd have her as well trained as her bears.

There were six more acts before the grand finale, a parade around the ring by all the acts. Madame Ursa and her bears were in the middle of the parade. The bears each pushed a clown riding in a brightly painted wheelbarrow. As they paraded around the circus circuit, clowns tossed confetti and streamers into the air. The bears ignored the confetti and streamers that landed on them, while they dutifully marched around the tent.

When the finale parade ended, the sheriff hurried out of the tent, dodged around his constituents, the circus workers, and ran to the back lot. He showed his badge to get past the roustabouts who guarded the performers' private quarters.

Madame Ursa helped her bears comb the confetti from each other's coats. She saw the sheriff coming. "Well, hello! Glad you made it. We'll be gone by sunrise. Are you sure you don't want to just let us move on?"

The sheriff stared at her with hard hungry eyes. "I'm sure."

She shrugged her shoulders. "Okay, your choice. I need a few minutes to get my boys down for the night. You might as well make yourself comfortable and wait in my trailer."

"Where's your trailer?" He blurted.

Madame Ursa pointed to a nearby purple and gold trailer. "Go inside and make yourself at home." She smiled. "I took the liberty of opening a bottle of wine. It's from my family vineyards. My sisters manage the family property on a small Greek island where we've made wine from the same recipe and same vines for longer than any of us can remember."

"I'll see you inside." Then he stopped. "Did you locate the ownership papers and vet records for the bears?"

She batted her eyes and shook her head from side to side. "I didn't even look for them. You don't really want to look at papers tonight, do you? Wasn't that only an excuse to spend time with me?"

The sheriff leered at her and grinned, "Yes, it was. You don't mind do you?"

"Would it matter if I did? You go on inside and pour yourself a glass of wine. There's a tray of fruit and feta cheese in the fridge. Help yourself, I'll be right there. The sooner I get my boys down for the night, the sooner we can relax. Save some wine for me."

The sheriff watched Ursa saunter away then hurried to the trailer, climbed the three steps, and opened the door. Long drapes and colorful tapestries covered the walls, oriental rugs lay about the floor, and glass beaded curtains hung in doorways. He entered the kitchen, found a fruit and cheese platter, and set it in on the table. He popped a small piece of cheese and a grape into his mouth and poured a glass of wine from the decanter. It was dark red, almost black. The sheriff swirled the wine a couple of times and took a long swig.

"A little sweet for my taste," he admitted to himself. "But better than that 'Single Star Beer' they make in the state capitol though." He nibbled a little more fruit, broke off another piece of cheese, and took another sip, then finished his first glass and poured himself another. The wine wasn't too sweet, it was actually perfect.

As he drank, he began to feel warmer. Madame Ursa said he should make himself comfortable, so he took off his shoes and utility belt. He put his hat on the counter, peeked out the door to check on Madame Ursa, finished his second glass of wine, and sat back down.

"Slow down, big boy," he told himself. "You don't want to be drunk when the little lady gets here, you want to enjoy tonight. One more little sip won't hurt though, and this is the best wine I've ever tasted." One more little sip led to one more glass. After the third glass, the sheriff felt light headed and started to itch all over, like he'd gone skinny dipping in a poison ivy patch. He stumbled against the table and bumped it across the kitchen to the wall. He lurched backwards and knocked over his chair.

"It's sure getting dark in here," he mumbled to the empty room. At least, I didn't spill the wine." When he reached for the chair, his head played roulette. The kitchen spun in circles around him. He sat on the floor and held his head to stop the carousel.

"I'll just rest for a minute," he mumbled, and that's when everything went black.

*

The sheriff awakened to the rumble of a diesel engine and the monotonous drone of tires on the highway. He found himself caged, inside a big trailer. The floor was covered with straw and sawdust. Five bears were caged across the floor. The place stunk. Windows were open along the sides of the trailer, allowing the circulation of fresh air. He sat up and reached to wipe his face with his right hand, but it wasn't a hand, it was a paw, a big black smelly bear paw with big black shiny bear claws. He held his fur covered arms out. Bear arms! He had bear arms, bear feet, bear legs, and bear fur. He was covered him from head to foot!

He tried to walk to the edge of his cage, but fell over. He didn't know how to use his body and he couldn't make it do what he wanted. He crawled to the side of the cage, nearest the other bears, and put his paws on the bars. A pitiful excuse for a growl escaped his mouth. He felt embarrassed by the weak *mew* sound he'd made. A bear with amber eyes raised one arm and waved. It was the royal wave, elbow, elbow, wrist, wrist, wrist. Queen Elizabeth would have been proud.

When the truck stopped, Madame Ursa came in with food and water. She handed a shovel and trash bag to each of the five bears so they could clean their own cages. Madame Ursa then stood with her hands on her hips in front of the sheriff. "Good morning. Looks like you've put on a little weight since last night. You could use a shave. What big teeth you have."

The sheriff's eyes were filled with horror. He gestured with his paws. Ursa laughed, "When you behave like an animal, you get to be an animal. I gave you a chance to go home." Her eyes were wide. "But instead, you used your authority to lord it over hard working folks just trying to make a living. Took their money. Forced women to do what you want. Double shame on you! You aren't a man, you're an animal." She practically kicked the cage, but refrained.

"You'll become more of a bear every day." She explained. "You'll always understand enough to do just what I tell you."

He pinned his eyes onto her shapely legs, her shifting hips and mocking upturned lip. "I told you," she leaned in, "I don't know how long my family's been making wine." She paused. "That's not true. My ancestress, Circe, developed the vintage over three thousand years ago. She used it to protect herself and her friends from drunken sailors, soldiers, and men like *you* who constantly showed up on her island, uninvited. She made them welcome, gave them a little smile, a little cheese, some fruit, and a flagon of her wine." The sheriff grew angry. "Welcome to the circus, where we make dreams come true seven shows a week." She said proudly. "We open tomorrow in Plainville. We'll rehearse once the Big Top and midway are set up for tonight's show."

*

Early the next season, the circus was scheduled for a three day show in Riverton. The Riverton mayor and his son visited the lot one morning before matinee time. With a box of dog biscuits and a sack of donuts, they approached Madam Ursa.. The ringmaster had promised the kid he could feed the animals. They watched Madame Ursa and her bears and the boy finally asked, "How come you got six bears?"

"Seven bears is too many and five isn't enough, young man."

"Can I feed them?"

"Of course you can feed them. See the one with the ice blue eyes? His name is Sheriff. He's my favorite." The sheriff glowered at her, but Madame Ursa continued in her sweet melodic voice. "He likes chocolate covered donuts the best. Go on, you can feed him. He doesn't bite."

Author's Bio:

Robert Allen Lupton is retired and lives in New Mexico where he is a commercial hot air balloon pilot. Robert runs and writes every day, but not necessarily in that order. More than seventy-five of his short stories have been published in several anthologies including the NYT best seller, "Chicken Soup For the Soul – Running For Good", and online at www.horrortree.com, www.crimsonstreets.com, www.aurorawolf.com, www.stupefyingstories.blogspot.com, www.fairytalemagazine.com, and www.allegoryezine.com. Over 350 drabbles based on the worlds of Edgar Rice Burroughs and several articles are available online at www.erbzine.com. His novel, Foxborn, was published in April 2017 and the sequel, Dragonborn, in June 2018. His collection of running themed horror, science fiction, and adventure stories, Running Into Trouble, was published in October 2017. His annotated edition of John Monro's 1897 novel, A Trip To Venus, was released in September 2018. His stories have received five honorable mention awards from "Writers of the Future." Read his blog at https://robertalllenlupton.blogspot.com/ .

Old Tony's *Smashing* Chair

By Paul Attmore

A damp leaf blown half dry by the autumn wind, scuttled on stage left. That's how Old Tony told it and he wasn't far wrong. But I'd say, my first time at The New Found Theatre was more of a winter wind blew me in than an autumn and more of a stumble on stage than a scuttle. I'd put my unhappy weight against the stage door and there I was — a bungled entrance, whichever way you look at it.

Old Tony would stand, dustpan and brush in hand, a startled gaze softening under the house lights. I'd slink backstage like an injured cat and when he'd find me pounding the crumbling plaster walls outside the Green Room, he'd wrestle me to the ground and roll me up in an old dusty curtain.

"I've got a suitcase like you," he'd say, kneeling on me as I'd try to wriggle free. "Won't do what you want unless you sit on the bugger. Now you listen to me, you're gonna stop hurting yourself and join Old Tony for a cuppa tea and an Eccles cake, all right?"

And then a little later, as the kettle that never seemed to switch off filled the box office with steam, he told me that the best place to put lost and broken things was inside The New Found Theatre. I'd wanted my heart to do nothing else but stop since Dad died. Yet Old Tony got me laughing at myself, simple as that. More than a father to me, he was. I never told him. Wish I had.

"Two minutes!" The words exit our director's nose with the velocity of a sneeze. Should be selling *Evening Standards* outside Borough Tube with a voice like that, not directing Hamlet. His name's Roland — Roland Hamm to be exact. You couldn't make it up.

Tonight's our dress rehearsal and I'm the actor pouring poison into the King's ear in front of Hamlet's uncle. Despite knowing Hamlet's lines better than Philippe, his cannabis smoking boyfriend, I'm playing another minor mute character during the so-called Dumb Show. All he ever gives me is non-speaking roles. I should be playing the unhappy prince. Better than most, I know his anger.

A month after Dad died, I found Uncle Simon and Mum at it on the kitchen table. The soles of Uncle Simon's feet looked as if he'd been dancing on coal and Mum was moaning — a higher, more pleasurable pitch than the usual groaning sounds she'd make at night, due to those nightmares in Dad's king size bed.

Old Tony told me they put on three amateur productions a year but, like I say, one of Roland Hamm's favorites I am not. When I auditioned for the part of Hamlet, he waved me away, before I could even tell Ophelia to get herself along to the nunnery.

"… I'm very proud, revengeful, ambitious," I said, thinking of Uncle Simon's blotchy ass pounding my poor mum. "With more offences at my back than I have time to put them in, imagination to give them shape, or —"

"Next!" Roland said, one eyebrow raised, little finger up his nose. He looked at me pitifully and told me I was too short to play Hamlet, then he sucked that fresh bogey finger like a lollipop.

Who says Hamlet's tall anyway? I know I'm only five foot six inches and look younger than my nineteen years, but I've grown a pencil thin moustache, so I can play older parts and get served in pubs without the third degree. I didn't tell Roland that. He put another finger up his nose and shooed me away as Philippe began flouncing around pretending to be mad with a fish slice.

I walk into something in the wings — Old Tony's *smashing* chair. Actors keep it handy to prop the stage door open during cigarette breaks. He used to call it his "*smashing*" chair because he liked it, not because he used it for smashing things up. Smashing meant fabulous. Collapsing into it after rehearsals, he'd sigh and say, "it's a smashing chair this." It's a beast of a chair, antique oak with a hard, unforgiving seat — nothing *smashing* about it, in my opinion. Ordinary, if you'd ask me. He said he got into the habit of saying the word *smashing* off some quiz show host on the telly, but I've never heard anyone use it apart from Old Tony. Yeah, that's right, Old Tony's gone too. A few days after Roland told him he'd given the part of Polonius to someone else, he was run over by a double-decker bus outside Sainsbury's. I'm not saying there's any connection, but one witness said he'd thrown himself under its wheels, another — an old woman with a shopping trolley, puffing on a long thin cigar — told me he'd slipped on a banana peel. She looked so serious when she said this. I couldn't help but laugh.

"Open the door a wee bit would you lad," says a weak ready voice in a Scottish accent. It's Douglas who's playing Polonius. I push the door open and jam the chair under the handle, flooding backstage with sunshine. Particles of dust twist in the light.

"Shut that bloody door! It's the dead of winter in Elsinore not a balmy spring day," yells Roland Hamm, who's more concerned about keeping Hamlet's winter scene intact

I kick the chair from under the handle, but as I grab it, someone shoves me roughly out the door, hurling the chair after me. The door slams shut and I drop to my knees, blinking in the spring sunshine. I try the handle and put my weight against the stage door, but unlike my first time at The New Found Theatre, it won't budge. I knock three times.

"Knock, knock, knock!" says some joker behind the door — Philippe by the sound of it, chuckling away with one of his slippery friends. "Who's there in the devil's name?"

That was one part Old Tony was born to play. The audience couldn't get enough of his drunken gatekeeper. I pull Old Tony's chair onto its feet and slump down like a sorry bag of spuds. It has one leg shorter than the others, so you need to put your weight forward or backwards to stabilize it. They say Old Tony was caught (once) masturbating in the wings during a production of *A Christmas Carol.* He was understudying Marley's ghost. Sometimes, behind closed doors in the bathroom, I'd hear him rocking it back and forth, the *lacklustre rhythm of a lonely loveless man.*

"Killswater!" Roland's furious voice is muffled behind the stage door. He always uses my surname — like the surly headmaster of some dreadful public school.

"Adieu, adieu!" I mumble, stand up, bow and walk away. I can't believe I'm doing this after three years, but with Old Tony gone, there's nothing much keeping me here. It seems leaving The New Found Theatre may be a slightly less bungled affair than my entrance.

*

Before I cross the busy main road on the way home, I stop outside the chip shop. Bob's fish and chips are pretty dodgy, but fried potato smells damn good right now. Bob shakes his head, when I pull on the door, and points to his watch. Not open for another hour, he mouths, a pink sausage dripping yellow batter from his pudgy hand. I make my way back in the direction of the small, dilapidated theatre — situated so close to the main road, the stage often vibrates when heavy vehicles drive by. I notice Old Tony's chair is still outside the stage door, so I pop back down the alley, insert my right arm between its robust legs and hoist it onto my shoulders.

With chair on my back, I decide it's best to avoid three lanes of traffic. I take the underpass: a sunless, piss-stinking passage that runs under the A2. It's where everything rotten seeps — an unofficial sewer for humanity and best avoided if you want to keep money in your pocket. Surely, even some brainless thug wouldn't be interested in an old chair — *smashing* or not.

Outside the entrance a breeze sends a plastic cup skidding towards a shit splattered bin overflowing with beer cans and crisp packets. Pink blossoms, fallen from a line of cherry trees on the road above, swirl around the threshold. I stop for a moment, take in the accidental poetry of this awful place, fix my gaze on the square of sunlight at the far end of the tunnel and walk straight ahead.

Halfway through, something hot warms my cheeks. An attractive girl, wearing a pink leather jacket and ripped jeans, steps across my path. Her black hair- fringe breaks across her forehead like a dark wave covering her right eye.

"I could do with a seat down 'ere." She wrenches the chair from me. I stagger forward grasping for it, but instead, fall to my knees as she pulls it out of reach. On the ground, I notice half a cigarette smouldering next to a puddle. I stand up and crush it underfoot.

"You want some shorty?" She bounces around me throwing punches, waggling a stud pierced tongue through cracked, red painted lips. When she weaves behind me, shuffling her feet and making whooping and whooshing noises, I climb onto the chair. She seems surprised and steps back, her rhythm broken.

"This is Old Tony's chair," I say.

She folds her arms. "Who's Old Tony?"

"Dead." I say. "He's dead." The echo in the underpass magnifies the frailty of my voice. A chick's first chirp through a crack in its egg — that's how Roland Hamm describes it. I remember Old Tony climbing onto his chair after rehearsals to regale us with his farfetched adventures as a merchant seaman. He had this deep voice — rough as a deckhand's scrubbing brush. His words, not mine. The chair creaks reassuringly beneath me now, like an old, but trusted ship.

"Good!" She bangs the sole of one scuffed winkle-picker against the graffiti-covered wall and turns away, looking sad.

"You knew him?" I ask.

"Course not prick! People come and people go that's all."

She's got some story; a brother stabbed by a gang outside the Polish off-Licence or a poor old mum dying slowly of cancer in a high rise. Something heart wrenching, but I say nothing and let the clatter of cars, tearing down the A2, fill the silence.

Old Tony once told me: you follow that road it goes all the way to the sea, then a boat to France and the world's your proverbial oyster young man. I thought about Dad when he told me that too. How he took us on a ferry across the English Channel to buy Christmas booze in Dieppe, where he bought us lunch in a little restaurant. I had French onion soup, followed by Crocque-Monsieur. Mum and Dad talked about him retiring from the army and buying some place in France. They were like that. Then he was off again, to Afghanistan this time— that's where a sniper took him down with a bullet through the back of his head. Truth is, I never knew him. Most of the time he'd come home, we'd kick a football around a bit, he'd get drunk with his brother, Uncle Simon, and he was off again.

The girl snorts, pulling snot into her mean mouth. "Fuck off and take that chair with you!" She spits, but her gob misses me and lands in the puddle.

I remember Mum pushing Uncle Simon off her, kneeling next to the cooker, buttoning up her blouse—adjusting her skirt back around her hips. I had swallowed my words then, went into the lounge and stuck the telly on full volume.

"I'm breaking free!" I shout and the passage seizes the words, fattens them up and pings the vibrating vowels and consonants against the concrete walls.

"All right Freddie Mercury, now do one!" She says.

"When I get home, I'm gonna tell Mum," I continue. "If Uncle Simon's home, I'll tell him too and do what he's been on at me to do since Dad died."

"Do one prick!"

"Exactly, I'm leaving." Old Tony's chair rocks back and forth beneath me. I stare into her cool blue eyes and lower my voice. "When Uncle Simon stopped screwing my mum, he got off her and stood, legs astride, trousers around his ankles, his hard cock withering in front of me —"

"Shut up! That's disgusting." She puts her hands to her ears and shakes her head as if the image of Uncle Simon naked has been locked inside and she's trying to get it out.

"He didn't seem bothered. Then he tells me, if I say anything to anyone he'll rip my tongue out."

"You're bonkers."

"He still made a point of watching every one of our performances, though," I continue — pitching my voice so it's soft and conversational. It seems to grab her attention. "Comes along to the theatre with Mum and tears it apart over a pint of Guinness and a packet of pork scratchings. Do you know *The New Found Theatre*?'

"No!" She yells.

"It's on the High street next to Bob's Fish and Chips. He did a television commercial for Lemsip way back. Uncle Simon, not Bob. He said nothing, but was superb at looking really ill. Reckons he's an expert on all things drama because of that." I pause and she stares silently back down the underpass.

"He's nothing like the guy in the advert — you could almost like that sorry, sniffling git. So yeah, I'm fucking off. I'm getting a place of my own with a kettle that switches off and doesn't boil dry. 'Alas, Old Tony! I knew him so well. A fellow of infinite jest, of most excellent fancy. He too stood upon this —"

She pushes herself away from the wall with her foot and pulls the chair from under me. I crash to the ground — my left cheek immersed in cold, putrid water. I close my eyes, but continue talking. You could say I've found my voice.

"Why wouldst thou be a breeder of sinners?" I say.

Her departing footsteps stop. Everything, even the traffic, halts on the road above. There's probably a red light at the pedestrian crossing near Sainsbury's where Old Tony bought it.

I wait for the girl's footsteps to start up again, to fade and leave. A huge vehicle thunders overhead, sending a gust of wind through the passage. Things are moving. I open my eyes to see her sitting crossed legged on Old Tony's chair — her black hair swept back from a white oval face revealing a purple bruise under her right eye. Pink blossoms, whipped up by the speeding lorry, fill the air, twist and turn in the half-light.

Her lips are pursed. Holding back anger, misery or joy, I can't tell so I stand up and give her my audition speech — all of it. She looks at me, mouth hovering between smirk and scowl, but her eyes huge, fixed on me.

"Get thee to a nunnery!" I say pitching my voice as deep as possible, ushering her away with the same lazy gesture Roland Hamm used to send me back into the wings. She sighs, drops her head allowing a dark, neatly cut fringe to cover her whole face and then the chair clatters to the ground behind her. Her head's thrown back and she's laughing like a nutter. She picks up the chair and sits on it the wrong way round, rests her chin on the top rail. Black mascara streaks across her porcelain skin. "Where's the local nunnery?"

I roll my eyes and suck my lips in. "I'll Google it." I say.

"Did he really stand there naked, this Uncle Simon with his cock out?" She whispers the word cock like a stuffy old aunt excited by the thought of it. "Yuck!'

"No, he covered his gonads with a dishcloth."

"Nice," she says and twists her mouth into an evil grin. "You wanna get him back?"

She's like Ophelia, but a mean and vengeful one with mud from the river blackening her long fingernails.

"What was it you said, revengeful?" She grinds a cherry blossom into the cement with her left boot. "Best served cold or something, isn't it, revenge?"

"I, dunno but I could really go for something warm right now. Do you fancy sharing a bag of chips down Bob's Chippy?" She looks a little taken aback. "I'm not really the bloody revenge type."

"You're buying!" she says. "I want mine with ketchup — loads. I guess I'm not really the revenge type either."

"Who hit you?"

"I'm more of a ketchup on my hands kind of girl than a blood." She pulls both legs to her chest, spins her body to the right and stands up. "My dad gets pissed and expressive with his fists. My brother used to stand up for me. He's gone."

"Where?"

"Joined the army."

"What's your name?" I ask.

She ignores me and walks back down the passage dragging the chair behind her.

"Leave it," I say.

She stops. "What?"

"The chair. Leave it here."

She places it against the wall of the underpass. "Here ok?"

"A little to the right," I say.

"Prick!" She pulls the chair away as I move to take it — just like she did before. I'm a little off balance, however, I'd fall. Not this time.

"Joking aside, I've got to do this."

Egged on by her whoops and whistles, I smash the chair against the wall of the underpass. It cracks, but holds its form. Still four legs and standing, a little askew. Over the head, I bring it down on the ground and it breaks in two — a sorry sight — then stamp upon the oak legs. I'd need a sledgehammer to break those thick stumps so I turn attention to the seat where so many times Old Tony stood telling his preposterous tales and sat singing some Elvis Presley hit.

After I'm done, the seat and legs still whole — none of it now connected — she kicks aside some shards of broken chair and says, "Feel like a rock star?"

"No."

"Chips?"

"Yep."

"Let's go."

"That hurt," I say.

She frowns. "Your hands?"

"No."

As we walk back down the passage, she begins to talk. It feels natural, unpractised, all of it —unrehearsed. I'm stuck on every one of her words! When we leave the underpass, the smell of fried potatoes greets us. She stops, pulls me close to her — her hands warm, her fingers long. "My name is Lisa," she says.

Author's Bio:
Paul Attmere is an actor and writer. Trained in mime and Commedia del Arte he has worked with theatre companies in both the UK and Europe and has an MA in Performance Making, from Goldsmiths' University, London. More recently he founded Third Knock Theatre Company and wrote and performed his first solo theatre performance, "Broken Air", inspired by Cornish artist Peter Lanyon.

Originally from the UK he now lives with his family in Krakes, a small town in Lithuania where he teaches English, writes and acts. He's been published in Spread the Word - Flight Journal.

Visit to the Cralnaw Estate

By Anthony Peters

I'm counting one, two…

Five…and seven. Wonderful!

Now that we have everyone here please gather around me. Gather around, gather around. Get real close now, and be sure to perk up those ears.

First of all, welcome to the Cralnaw Estate! I'll be your guide on this tour. If you get separated from the main group, which, let me stress, should not happen, please keep an eye out for the tour's banner. I will be holding that banner, and you can follow it to rejoin the group.

Second, I will now pass out the tour shirts. As you can see each one is a single color, and I will refer to the color of your shirt, if I need to address you. Since the opening of the estate to the public, we receive a near constant stream of guests, and it can be difficult to remember names in a pinch. Through trial and error we have found this to be the easiest method for everyone.

Yes Chartreuse? Yes, the shirts are mandatory. I'm sorry Chartreuse, but we don't have time for silly questions. The timer started as soon as I handed out the shirts. Now before we proceed through the front doors, I need everyone to arrange themselves single file behind me.

*

That went well. I love people that can organize! It means I won't have to whip out the banner. *I hate the banner.* As some of you may know, entering the estate used to be quite the process. Baron Bartholomew Cralnaw was considered to be an eccentric by many of his contemporaries, and he employed several methods to guarantee that he would receive only predestined visitors. Of course most of these methods have been disabled by estate curation, due to safety concerns, but we still keep a few around to add some flavor to your experience.

For example, observe this lovely door knocker. Does anyone know the passcode? I'm excited to hear that Periwinkle! By all means, please demonstrate.

Excellent, glad to see that someone has done their homework! Baron Cralnaw had notable interests in both astrology and coded communication, and one of the ways he married these passions was by making his passcode the current month's current sign, and by having that sign knocked out in Morse code. You might think this to be a bit of a hassle, but Bartholomew felt very protective of his collections.

And right on cue, it sounds like the deadbolt has been lifted! Follow me, please. We are now in the entryway, or as the gentry would have called it at the time: the foyer. Notice the delicate crown molding, the astrological signs subtly carved into the columns, and of course, the reams of brilliant pink carpet. It reminds me of you, Fuchsia!

No Fuchsia, you cannot switch shirts with Mauve. I'm sorry to inform everyone that the shirt situation is pretty much permanent. If we can all understand that, perhaps we can accept our lots in life and move on.

Look everyone, here comes First Floor Butler. Everyone wave to First Floor Butler. Of course that's not the butler's actual name

Ochre, don't be ridiculous. The butlers are a quiet sort, and keep that information to themselves. Therefore, we name them according to the floor they reside on. We're all about efficiency on the curation committee.

Oh look what we have here! It appears that the First Floor Butler has two scrolls. Who could those be for, I wonder?

My, my. Congratulations Ochre and Chartreuse! No need to be so bashful; the Butler won't bite... yet. Kidding, I'm just kidding everyone. I've got to work on my material somewhere, right?

Go on, read the scrolls! For heaven's sake, it looks like the poor dears can't parse Pig Latin. Please help them, Periwinkle. Before the tour began, we selected two guests to partake in the Mystery Tour, and you are our lucky winners! Please follow First Floor Butler to the end of the hall, where you will be handed off to Basement Butler to start your special tour. And remember, we want to preserve the wonder for all future guests, so please consult the NDAs you signed before spoiling the fun. We'll catch up with them later. Follow me please, and we'll make our way up the stairs.

*

This climb to the second floor takes longer than you'd think, so I like to take this time to remind everyone of how much effort the curation committee has put into restoring this mansion to its original glory. Without their hard work, well, let's just say the upper floors would still be off limits. Of course the Estate Research Institute has been crucial to cataloging new discoveries, and let us not forget about Cralnaw's butlers. When the Baron passed, if we hadn't been given their blessing, this whole place would still be under lock and key!

Notice the smell in the air as we ascend. It's subtle, but what you are detecting is a heady mixture of glutaraldehyde, methanol, and of course, formaldehyde. It's a little known fact, but after he stopped leaving the estate, Baron Cralnaw took a keen interest in the art of embalming. As for why, no one really knows. Perhaps in mastering the art of preservation, he thought to better understand death, and through that understanding, glean his way around it.

No reason to blanch, Burgundy. The man *clearly* did not succeed.

We'll be getting off here, at the first landing. As I'm sure you've already gathered from the echoes of your footsteps, the floor switches from carpet to marble. Much like his hobbies, Cralnaw's taste in decor was esoteric, and did not always follow the traditional layout. We will see more of that later. This door has a low frame Charcoal, so you might need to stoop a bit.

I can tell from the smiles that this is more what you've been hoping to see! Cralnaw called this space the Dining Hall, but we here on the curation committee have taken to nicknaming it the Pallid Room. I always enjoy taking guests through here, because the tour shirts really make the room "pop". In accordance with Baron Cralnaw's wishes, we have placed a preserved specimen of his at each seat of the table. Set it up a bit like *The Last Supper.* An inside joke by *management, as it were.*

Now, does anyone spot a pattern? Lower your hand, Periwinkle. Nobody likes a show-off. You've been awfully quiet, Mauve. What do you think? Here's a hint: midnight.

Very astute! Once you notice it, every instance starts to jump out. Look at the columns. Now look at the windows. Do you recall the First Floor Butler's tattoo? The number is everywhere!

Okay, time for one of my favorite activities. This might sound a bit kooky, but humor me. I want everyone to make their way to one of the seated figures. Pick the one that interests you, the one that quickens your pulse. Has everyone made their decisions? Good. Now touch them. Just with your fingertips. Think of that which you must know over all else. Now place an ear by their mouths, as if listening for a breath. Closer. Well? Pretty cool right?

I'm sorry Burgundy, not everyone hears something. There will be several more hands-on activities on the tour, so don't worry. You'll have many more opportunities.

Speak of the devil, here comes Second Floor Butler to hand out the semaphore flags. At least you're not that tall, right Charcoal? Yes Mauve, these are the weird boat flags that sailors wave, as you so elegantly put it. Please stop twirling your pair. You'll poke someone's eye out.

If everyone has their flags, we will follow Second Floor Butler down the hall to the back of the mansion. Please do not drop the semaphore flags, and please do not touch the displays hung up in the hall. They are very old, and prone to collapse.

As we make our way to the Library, you might have noticed the interesting texture of the walls. Cralnaw became a little obsessed with embalming near the end of his life, and began to believe he could preserve stranger things than animals with the right technique. He began to synthesize new mixtures, pulling from both experimental chemicals and old texts. At one point he even began to embalm the house, and the bloated, soggy wallpaper here is the result of his tampering. You didn't hear it from me, but I think the loneliness started to get to him.

Careful, Burgundy. No, these displays won't speak to you if you touch them. *Especially* not that one. I'm very serious about the no-hands policy. Stop! Don't make me pull out the banner. I know how empty it makes you feel. You'll recover, I promise. Think of the gift shop. Nothing soothes my nerves like picking up some fridge magnets for the nieces and nephews.

Here we are: Library. Please make your way around Second Floor Butler's tail, and crane your necks to take in the view. Baron Cralnaw read in this library until his mysterious death, and it was from these tomes that many of his interests and fascinations had their inception. The first shelf contains mostly literature, but going up we have poetry, scientific essays, folders of floor plans, encyclopedias of pagan symbols, binders of cipher analysis, sketchbooks of animal skeletons, and at the very top, the recipe files. Perhaps most fascinating are the books he hid behind the shelves, but you are not the right tour for those. Follow me through the brass double doors on the left. Uh oh: they're locked! Hmmm, how do you think we could open it? I wonder if it has something to do with your semaphore fl-

Jesus Christ Burgundy! Don't touch the butler! Burgun—

*

Fuchsia, if you are going be sick, please make sure none of it gets on the rugs.

I'm so sorry about that, Second Floor Butler. You saw how I tried to stop Burgundy from touching your scaly skin. Burgundy had eyeballs, he should have been able to tell what you could do to him. He just couldn't keep his hands to himself, and look where it got him: murdered in cold blood! You're heading down to the basement? Please, please don't report me. You can have the rest of Burgandy if you don't report me.

Charcoal, would you please pick Burgundy's flags up off the ground before they get soaked with his blood? I'll use them for the exercise.

Yes Mauve, I understand why you would feel that way. Do not worry; we are in very good hands here. It's just that there are rules, and it is best to follow them. Let this be a lesson: don't touch anything! Back to the demonstration. Can I have the flags, Charcoal? Thank you.

Frequent visitors to the estate became quite familiar with its cozy, if not strange smelling, halls. However, there were things that

Cralnaw kept from even his closest friends. Take for example, the third floor. It is a place that appears on no floorplan of the house, and due to the thick layer of fog covering the property, one cannot even detect its presence from the outside. But I assure you, it is most certainly there.

The Estate Research Institute didn't even discover the floor's existence, until 30 years after Bartholomew Cralnaw's supposed death, and then only because the faint skittering from Third Floor Butler was it given away. By careful study of the Baron's notes, we have pieced together how he first made contact with the butlers: semaphore. Thus, by applying this knowledge with some of the clues left in this library, we have figured out how to gain access to the third floor. Normally we give visitors some of those same clues, and see if you all can figure it out on your own. However, in light of Burgundy's demise, I imagine everyone might need a bit of a breather. Therefore, I'll approach the door and just sign out the code with the flags.

O-Z-Y-M-A-N-D-I-A-S

It is most certainly *not* like waving pom-poms, Charcoal! Semaphore is a revered and time-honored tradition, with specific flag positions indicating specific letters. You try spelling out S.O.S. with pom-poms the next time you're on a sinking ship and let me know how that works out for you. Enough comments from the peanut gallery, we need to shuffle through the door before it closes again. It can't be opened from the other side, and I would hate to leave anyone near the Pallid Room alone.

Everyone in? One, two, three, four. All right, you guys are rock-stars at this! I can't believe with a group so good that a murder in the Library could happen. Must have been a fluke. Watch your steps as you ascend the ladder. The lighting isn't great on the third floor, and I'd hate for anyone to get a splinter.

Periwinkle, would you be *so* kind as to pass me a torch from the rack? I'll light it from the brazier. This floor hasn't been fully renovated yet, and is a bit rough around the edges. Take for example, the lack of electricity. Even without our renovations, it is clear that Cralnaw didn't care much for the third floor. Gone are the filigree animals from the chandeliers, and even his trademark braille wallpaper has been skinned from the walls. When we move away from the brazier, you might notice a drop in temperature. Baron Cralnaw never installed insulation up here, and as for why, we can only speculate. I suspect the chill kept his wits sharp.

Hmm, looking at my watch, it appears like we have less time than I thought. I think I'm going to take us on a shortcut, through the Shrouded Gallery. Any objections to arriving at the elevator early? Didn't think so. I don't know about you, but this place gives me the willies.

As we walk please take a moment to familiarize yourselves with the lions etched upon the stone underfoot. If you become separated from the group, locate the Lion path as soon as possible. It connects the library to the elevator, which will take us back to the first floor. Just make sure you follow it in the right direction. The way back is shut, and Second Floor Butler isn't very talkative, after what he did to Burgundy.

Funny you should ask, Fuchsia. That is the first question we had about the third floor, and it is still one of the last unanswered. We suspect that at some point deep into his research of immortality, Baron Cralnaw covered up all the mirrors. As we enter the Shrouded Gallery, notice that it follows the same pattern. Whenever I walk through here, I can't help but wonder what drove Cralnaw to this. Did he comb literature to find the secret to eternal life, when science failed him? *The Picture of Dorian Gray* came out in the Baron's lifetime, and I believe that the novel resonated with him. After all, being preserved in art is its own kind of immortality, but perhaps Cralnaw didn't want to take any chances, and covered the portraits after their completion.

To mix in a little philosophy, if a painting is covered and nobody is there to witness it, who can claim it ages? Pulling off the shroud would answer that question of course, but what's the fun in that? Just between us, if all it took to live forever was transferring your soul to a portrait, I'd do it in a heartbeat. I hope it goes without saying, but please don't lift any of the fabric. We don't want another *Burgundy* incident. The butlers can get testy when touched. For that matter, don't stare down the neighboring halls we are passing. The torch casts long shadows on the old furniture. It might make you see things that are not there. Now another interesting thing about the gallery and the third floor in general, is that it gives us our first inklings of insight into what Cralnaw called in his journals *The Ecstasy of Liminali*——Sssshhhhh, no one move, nobody speak.

Mauve, what did it sound like? I heard nothing, but my hearing has been going since I visited the basement. Did it sound like clacking, like a dog on tile? Blink once for yes, twice for no.

Alright, change of plans. We are taking a detour on the Scorpion Path. Try to tread lightly on the stone, and keep your voices low until I say otherwise. Just so we're clear, I'm not scared. Nor do I think we are in any danger. I just feel like after the event on the previous floor, it might be best to avoid a meet-and-greet with Third Floor Butler.

Now through this room, lots of furniture, so don't trip over it. Avoid that floorboard; it squeaks. We are now entering the Hall of Silent Dance, no we are not. We are turning around and going towards the Grand Kitchen. Please don't look back it isn't following us, it's more scared of us than we of it. As you can see, the kitchen hasn't been used in some time, hence the spiders. Oh dear, it does appear to be following us, no time to stop. Pick up the pace please pick up the pace! Mauve I told you not to trip on the furniture! Leave her, I threw her the torch she'll be fine we need to go hustle! Everybody hustle!

And like that, we're at the elevator. Whew, I really got my steps in for the day! Didn't even have to whip out the banner. Just in case any of you are concerned, Mauve will be totally okay. The torch should discourage Third Floor Butler from pulling his usual antics. In the most remote chance that Mauve has perished, I will personally send her family some lovely carnations from the gift shop, along with my heartfelt condolences. That being said, I hope you all enjoyed your time at the Cralnaw Estate. Please take the time to fill out a suggestion card before you leave. We really appreciate them. Now let me just punch in my code for the elevator here, and we'll be on our—— oh....no —-Periwinkle, I didn't do that. It appears as if someone is already using the elevator, and they're coming from the basement. We don't have much of a choice, but to see. I think I speak for everyone when I say that going back towards the Lion path is bad news.

It looks like the elevator is here. I hope it's Butler-free.

Oh. *Oh.* Well cross my O's and call me the Zodiac Killer! It's our old friend Chartreuse! I hope the Mystery Tour was to your satisfaction. How did you feel about the photo-op? Haha, that's what I've heard! Hold on a second. What's that yellow strip peeking over your collar? That's not your undershirt. Don't bullshit me. And come to think of it, where's Ochre?

Grab him, Charcoal.

Just what I thought, that's Ochre's shirt. Explain yourself. And why should I believe the words of a shirt thief? You have me there. Not like you'll find me checking the basement to confirm your story. The butlers down there haven't been socialized. Insurance costs, I'm sure you all can understand. Also, I hate to burst your bubble Chartreuse, but you in fact do not absorb Ochre's life-force by wearing his shirt. I'm sorry, that's just not how life-force works.

Yes, yes, Fuchsia, we need to hurry, I know. No need to quiver. It's embarrassing. Okay so with everyone in, we will be taking the elevator down to the first floor.

Which wise guy pressed floor eleven? No one? You seem pretty on top of things Periwinkle: any funny business? No?

Hmmm, it appears the other buttons have become unresponsive. I've heard about this happening once before, but it was before my time. Actually right before my time, come to think of it. Stop trying to touch Charcoal's shirt, Chartreuse. Everyone focus, what I'm about to say is very important. We will be entering butler territory. Stay close to me. Don't make eye-contact with any of the butlers. We make for the stairs at the opposite end of the chamber. They lead to floor twelve, which the Estate Research Institute understands to be the top floor of the mansion. From there we will make our way down the fire-escape, taking our chances in the basement Additionally, I recommend breathing through your mouths, as the scent of formaldehyde is quite strong. Everything clear?

Good. Stay behind me as the doors open. No Charcoal, this is in fact very unusual. I've never known it to be so misty. You can't even see the ceiling.

Yes Fuchsia, there's a lot of them. We believe this is where the butlers spawn, that Baron Cralnaw found them up here, and it was because of their existence that he delved into his arcane practices. Who knows, perhaps the butlers found him. No more talking, not until we reach the end. The floor boards are rotten with preserving fluid, so step where I step…

Creak, creak, Creaaaak,shuffle, sniff, snniifff, Snnniiiiifffff. Clomp, clomp. Clomp. Clomp. CLOMPCLOMPCLOMP! I'll hold them back!

The stairs are that way! Don't lose each other in the darkness! Now *Run!*

*

Can I lean on you for a moment, Periwinkle? Sorry, but using the banner really takes it out of me. Phew. How'd we do? I see Chartreuse, Fuchsia, Periwinkle, Char...Charcoal? Where's Charcoal? How did you guys let her slip away? That's a fair point. We really should decommission the darker shirts. This is not the first time they have been a problem. The banner will need to take a few hours to recharge, so until then, Charcoal is on her own. Luckily she's big, almost as big as the butlers. If any of us have a chance, it's Charcoal.

I'm sure everyone wants to wrap things up, and fortunately the fire-escape should be close. Follow Periwinkle and me, if you please.

Yes Fuchsia, the smell is most pronounced up here. The board suspects that it seeps from Baron Cralnaw's crypt, up on floor twelve, at the end of all things. Rumor has it that the crypt door has been open as of late...Ugh, I'm going to need to get this checked out. To speed things up, could everyone please run their hands along the wallpaper? There's a hidden door around here somewhere, behind Baron Cralnaw's star sign.

Oh, what's that? Periwinkle found the door? I suppose I shouldn't be surprised. Where was it? Behind the sign of Ophiuchus? I should have known Baron Cralnaw would pull something like that. Clever bastard. Chartreuse and Fuchsia, go ahead and take the fire-escape. I don't want to slow you two down. Besides, Periwinkle has kindly volunteered to stay behind and escort me. Don't worry, I'll be fine. If you really want to brighten my day, you can give me a mention in your review. Management keeps tabs on those.

You too. Have a pleasant rest of your day. Enjoy the gift shop!

*

So, did I ace the performance review Periwinkle? I'm glad to hear that, sir. My only regret was not being able to have everyone figure out the semaphore puzzle. I know how much you like that part. Although if I recall right, this is the first review where we've had a hiccup like that. All things considered, that's not too shabby, right?

No, I don't think those two ever realized it. Fuchsia left too scared to think straight, and Chartreuse is, well... you saw how Chartreuse was right? I wanted to say something, like "I couldn't help but notice that you've stuffed Ochre's shirt down your pants," but the man seemed too far gone. Caught him eyeing Fuchsia's shirt as well. Probably solves that potential problem for us too, come to think of it.

Well, I suppose I need to be on my way. I'm not exactly in top form here, so walking down what I hope to be only eleven flights of stairs will take a bit. No, no, I think I can make it by myself. I appreciate the consideration, but you should return to your crypt, get some rest. I know how taxing these excursions can be for you. Although if I am to be so bold, I think I've earned an early retirement. Thank you Periwinkle, or should I say "Baron Cralnaw." Your understanding and vision know no bounds. Speaking of, I noticed the elevator had a new button. I'm surprised you didn't skip number 13. Many buildings do. May I ask when that floor will be open? Wonderful, simply wonderful. I can't wait for the next tour to see it.

Free Money

By Andrew Adams

Edward Meade was finishing breakfast, when his favorite hundred dollar bill tried to escape again. It was hard enough worrying about his friends and acquaintances coming into his house and walking away with his money, but of recent, it had started to walk away on its own. Instead of calling a security company, which he knew would take away even more of his money, Edward had developed his own system of keeping his money in check. He had put as many bills as he could in his wallet, since the money did not seem to have enough strength to unfold the wallet and slip out, at least when the wallet was in his pocket, wedged against his thigh and the cloth of the pants. For this very reason, he slept with his pants on, with wallet in pocket.

The other methods he developed were through trial and error. After the first three twenty dollar bills had escaped, Edward had placed a stack of them, bound together with a fat rubber band, in a birdcage hanging from the kitchen ceiling. The next morning, he took the money down and counted it, noticed that one of the bills had escaped, had carefully extracting itself from the rubber band, then slipped through the wide gaps between the bars of the birdcage. With duct tape, he wrapped these bills around his arm for the day and threw the birdcage out of the window. It was only when he heard the sharp clang and screech, seven stories and one cement conclusion below, that he realized he'd left his parakeet Felix in the cage. Instead of regretting his error and mourning his former pet, Edward decided Felix should have called for his attention when that twenty dollar bill had escaped the night before, and that death was a fitting punishment for sleeping on the job.

One of Edward's chief methods of monetary imprisonment was to put weights on top of the bills. He started with dumbbells of twenty - five pounds and this worked well, until he realized he was spending all his money on dumbbells. He got cheap and used what he had around the house to weigh the money down: stacks of books, chair legs, a bed, sofa, his TV, his dresser, his desk. He knew that tears and rips in his bills did not decrease their value, so he nailed some down. They easily escaped this way though, tearing themselves a bit more, like a fox who would bite off its own leg to escape ensnarement.

Edward didn't know where the money was going, but suspected his friends. Money could go a lot of places. It could go to the bank, the roads, or even to charity. If it weren't for his justified paranoia that his money would escape while he was gone, Edward would search his friends' houses for the money that had left him, keeping an eye out for those twenties with centralized stigmata, or he'd just look for his earmarks.

Edward had started marking all his money with the initials E.M. in his own nearly illegible handwriting. People had told Edward he had the handwriting of a doctor, which he found stupid, because there was no way the people giving away drugs at the pharmacies could read his handwriting. The E and the M looked like a spider dancing with a lightning bolt, but it only mattered that Edward recognized his initials.

Because of his obsession, Edward had been let go of his job and since he didn't own his apartment, money would be disappearing anyway. When his landlord came by for the rent, Edward sighed, picked up one of the twenty - five pound dumbbells, and watched as the money walked over to the landlord, climbed up his legs and torso and arms and into the man's hands.

Soon enough, Edward was down to his last ten bills. He had four hundreds, three twenties, a ten, a one, and a five. His favorite bill was the one hundred dollar bill, which was in the best condition. It was also his favorite bill because it never tried to escape. Having nothing left to lose, except all the remaining cash, Edward put the bill on the kitchen table and watched it. It did not even flutter to stretch out its watermark. It lay there like a loyal piece of green currency. Edward watched it all day and instead of putting it back under a weight, left it out when he went to bed. It was still there in the morning. Edward thought his luck had changed, so he took the weight off one of the twenties, which quickly sprinted across the floor, jumped onto the window sill, and sailed right out of the cracked window.

Edward left the weights on the rest of the bills.

But he did not put weight back on the one hundred. He ate with it and talked with it, since he had no more friends left. He laughed with it, even picked it up and kissed the dead freemason on the front. But one morning, as he was finishing breakfast, he saw it start to flutter in his periphery. When he looked back at the bill it was still. He was not sure if his mind was playing tricks on him because money walking out of his life was ridiculous enough already. He looked away and took a sip of his coffee and saw it flutter again.

The fluttering stopped when he pinned his pupils directly on it. It did not make any sense. Was the dollar bill slow to catch on or was it just growing tired of Edward? Or maybe, despite its monetary value, it was a baby just learning to walk. Edward didn't buy it. The bill was smarter than the others and that's why it was his favorite. It had planned this all along, gained Edward's trust, and now meant to screw with him and then leave him for good. Edward couldn't have that happen.

He reached under the table for a twenty - five pound dumbbell and when he lifted his head up the bill was gone. He jerked his head around and saw it slipping away, under the front door. He opened the door and chased the bill down the hallway, then down the stairway, then out through the lobby of the building. The bill jumped into a storm drain, which Edward was too big to squeeze through. He found a manhole above the drain, pried it open, nearly breaking his fingers in the process, and climbed down into the dank, dirty, darkness of the sewer.

While he waded through gunk, he saw the bill flying a ways ahead, as if it were Aladdin's magic carpet. When he couldn't see his money anymore, he could feel it. He used this force of greed and possession within, to follow the bill through a mile of sewage where it led him into a corner. He was finally out of the muck, stepping on solid ground. He noticed the bill right by his feet, as if waiting for him, but it was too dark to see anything else. Edward reached to his side and found a wall, then slowly dragged his hand against the wall and felt a switch, heavy as a circuit breaker. He pulled it. The room lit up and tiny green houses and cars and trees filled the room. It took Edward a minute to realize they were all made up of money.

Edward looked down at his hundred dollar bill, who beckoned him forward. He took a step and one of the houses exploded into the air, then flew towards Edward. He quickly turned to cover his face, using his arms as protection. He felt his hundred dollar bill pulling on his crusty pant leg. Edward uncovered his eyes and saw a huge stack of hundred dollar bills floating in the air. Although the hundred dollar bill didn't say a word, Edward knew what to do. He took the stack of money and put it in a clean bag that was lying on the ground. Then he climbed a ladder up to the real world, and looked down at his old friend, his favorite hundred dollar bill. Until next time, he thought.

When he got home he lifted the weight off his old money and it ran away immediately. He left his new stack of money out on the kitchen table and let it go wherever it wanted to.

Author's Bio:

Andrew Adams is happy to be publishing with Running Wild Press yet again. He lives in New York where he pursues acting and writing full time, with the exception of the survival gigs which only continue to reinforce his idea that living to merely survive is overrated. He is grateful, however, for the 14-hour night shift where he wrote the current story, "Free Money."

Creach

By Monique Gagnon German

We assumed we were alone, and we liked it that way. Our days were our own, feeding the animals, leading them across the pasture to graze and grow. Our nights were full of good chow and chatter, Craig, me, and the kids sharing stories from our afternoon adventures over chili and potatoes. There was no indicator that things would change, no sign from the sky, no difference in the air to signify the arrival of anything not us. It just happened one day, unseen, from somewhere quite close.

Kara was the one who caught it. She had it swaddled in the bottom half of her tattered favorite man-in-the-moon T-shirt. She hammocked her find in the fabric against her belly. When she lowered the shirt edge, I could see more of it. It was so new that its eyes were still sealed shut. I watched it squirm and try to maw at everything by throwing its wobbly head around in small arcs. It was hairless and gray. It almost looked like a newborn bird, but no beak. It had a mouth full of soft, grass-like teeth, and it purred, until Kara moved suddenly, then it shrieked. Kara swore it had to be friendly. "Just look how cute!" she said, trying to put a finger under its soft serrated claw. *Would that harden in time? And maybe also that meadow of teeth?*

Craig took a look when he got home. He wanted to cut it up and bury it immediately. "Doesn't belong here with us," he said real quiet. He meant it. Kara didn't hear him in her excitement to name the squirming thing. After everyone went to sleep, Craig took it out. I didn't stop him.

Kara realized it first thing the next day—that the new baby she'd named, "Creach," was gone! She darted from room to room to porch. "Where did it go!" she yelled, waking Link up. Link rubbing his eyes while not even awake, immediately knew. He said, "Pap must've kicked it out." Kara, with her messy hair, sweaty from searching, stopped suddenly in her tracks when she heard this. Her face paled with realization. She turned to her father. Her eyes squinted with rage and words came out of her mouth before she could stop them. "I hate you, you always take everything away!" She turned on her toes, which made the rubber soles of her Keds pipe an ear-startling high squeak as she ran the length of hall to the front door and burst through it to get away from us. The screen punched the frame behind her, adding a second exclamation point.

She wasn't exactly wrong, I thought for a second. We had gotten rid of a lot to move here, to live this way, far from the city's crimes, shootings, protests, and chaos. Her old friends, her old school, her old room had all been sacrificed by that choice. *But we couldn't exactly keep it, could we*, was my next thought right behind it. That thing couldn't be some sort of consolation prize, it was too dangerous.

When Kara came back, it was later than she'd ever stayed out before. Her fingernails were black moons from digging out in the woods, probably looking for it. Her face was brown-streaked from dirt and tears. I didn't let her get to the stairs, without getting in front of her and holding her in a hug for a minute. She stood still. She let me, but I didn't feel her arms in their usual spot around my waist. I said what I thought was most important. "I love you, Kara, you know your Pap makes these decisions to keep us safe." I wanted her to remember that most of all, I guess. The intent. She didn't answer. She just slowly pulled away and drifted upstairs to bed.

In the weeks that followed, Link searched our acres high and low, wondering where that thing got off to, after his father had set it free. Link swore to Kara that he'd find it or another one they could keep in secret, a pet of their own. He pinky promised. He was a good brother. I heard them plotting into the night, whispering confidantes. He told her they'd hide it in the barn in a cigar box under the hay. He was sure they could pull it off. "Trust me," he kept saying. "We'll get another one and make sure Pap never finds out!"

But honestly, I didn't like that thing from day one. It was a mutation of god knows what, probably carrying germs or diseases that could infect us all. I couldn't see a good outcome. I didn't like the idea of killing it off, but also didn't like the idea of that creature hanging around and gaining numbers. When I tried to picture that baby-thing grown up, I couldn't imagine it being friendly. The way it lurched and snapped its head at everything and those soft jagged teeth and claws, how easy to imagine them turning razor sharp—a baby, which would only going to grow hungrier and more threatening.

Even after Craig got rid of it, I was as nervous as he about the idea others might be lurking around. We'd talked about it into the wee hours. Craig said he'd try to find them all. Make sure none of them sneaked up on us bigger and angrier later, when we wouldn't expect them anymore. But we never found the mother or any others. If the horses, cows, or goats ever saw them, they never spooked or even got their hackles up. After weeks of secret searching, the kids seemed to finally give up and go back to hide and seek with each other, catching crickets, geckos, beetles and lightning bugs. Sometimes, Kara would put her insects-found in a jar full of grass and leaves and poke holes in the lid at the top. She'd talk to the little guys for a while. But she always let them go again, back to the safety outside our house.

We are alone again, just us. For now, anyway. The image, though, of that small "Creach," whether it could have been friendly or not still haunts. I'm wondering, after all, if we should have gotten rid of it like that, so unaware of what it even was. I wonder if it had a mother out there somewhere worrying about its outcome. But Craig said it was right to kill it off. That the thing didn't belong here, and no good could come of it, especially down the road. He might be right. But what if it wasn't like that? What if that thing had a purpose, a message for us?

For the past month since it's been gone, like clockwork I'm awake before dawn. I think about the things we've done to stay safe, how this way we live has changed all of us. Our house just isn't the same anymore. There is a silence behind the daily chores that feel full of something else. I think about Kara a lot, that look on her face when she yelled at her father. I know I can't un-change what's changed inside her, I can only worry what it might become. She hasn't been the same around him since that night. She talks a little like her old self before that fight, but not about the important things, what she's thinking or feeling. When Craig asks what she's gotten lately in her jars, she says, worms, or ants, or…"A frog," so carefully now. No excited chatter. And he only shows what she's got when he asks, she never invites. When it's time for bed, she hugs him, but never kisses him goodnight. Link still does, though. He acts like nothing's changed at all. I hear him sometimes talking to Kara, telling her she needs to forgive and move on. I can't hear her answers, but her tone says it all — rapid whispers launched like venomous snake strikes. She just wants it back, the squirming unknown. No matter the risks or costs.

Author's Bio:

Monique Gagnon German's poetry and fiction has appeared in over 35 journals/anthologies including: Rosebud, California Quarterly, Tampa Review, Off the Coast, The Ilanot Review, and The Wayfarer. Monique is a Pushcart Prize nominee. Her flash-fiction and short stories have been featured in: Kalliope, A Journal of Women's Literature & Art, The MacGuffin, and Adelaide Literary Review. For more Monique: http://moniquegagnongerman.webs.com/

Inglorious Carnage

By Jason Zeitler

No one was more vocal than Mrs. Parks about the recent explosion of ground squirrels in the neighborhood. She was the president of the Homeowners Association and for weeks had been hounding people to address the problem, which she insisted was due to the previous year's unseasonably warm winter. She never failed to complain, whenever she had a chance. Today, on the street outside her house, she happened to bump into two of her neighbors, while retrieving the mail: Mr. Douglas and Mr. Krieg. The first words out of her mouth were a sardonic remark about the weather. She admitted that last winter Tucson had been a paradise on earth, but she sounded more irritated than pleased by this. In her characteristic cynicism, she said nothing good comes without a cost, at the very mention of which her voice became grave, as if she were referring to the effects of an Ebola outbreak. She stopped and looked at the neighbors to gauge their reactions. They met her gaze with faces of stone, but she wasn't deterred. Shading her eyes with a hand, she peered up into the blistering June sun, then turned back to the two men with a look of utter disgust on her face. "Now we're paying the price," she said vaguely, and she stood there staring with unease at the myriad holes and mounds dotting the common areas along the street.

Mr. Douglas needed no prompting from Mrs. Parks. He was livid about the "little bastards," as he so peevishly referred to the ground squirrels. He called for immediate action. "Something's got to be done. At first I thought they were cute, but that was before they started ransacking my driveway." His voice faltered. Then he said, "See what I mean?" and he pointed with a trembling hand toward his house. Near the garage, where the squirrels had excavated a network of tunnels, several sections of paving stones were completely caved in, appearing to the untrained eye as if they'd been hit by an earthquake.

Upon seeing the damage, Mr. Krieg guffawed, his dark sense of humor getting the better of him. "Good Lord," he said, slapping Mr. Douglas on the back. "I had no idea it was as bad as all *that*." He wasn't exaggerating his ignorance. He could be oblivious in matters in which he wasn't directly concerned, a fault his wife Eileen was constantly berating him for. Now, as if seeing things for the first time, he took in the dire state of his neighbors' yards. Entrance after entrance to the squirrels' burrows lined the gravel paths skirting the road. He was reminded of the prairie-dog colony he'd seen on a recent trip to the Desert Museum. He wondered how the squirrels had done it all so quickly. It seemed to him they'd tunneled their way through the neighborhood practically overnight!

"So what do you propose we do about it?" asked Mrs. Parks, frowning at Mr. Krieg as if *he* were somehow to blame. But he didn't respond. He continued to look in disbelief at the handiwork of the squirrels, even as Mrs. Parks' question hung on the air like an accusation.

*

In the coming days, Maximus Krieg, as the secretary and lowest-ranking officer of the HOA, was tasked with finding a solution to the rodent problem. He was the logical person for the job. He was a school teacher, it was summer break, and he had an overabundance of time on his hands. Or so the thinking went. All the HOA members agreed that the first priority was to "deal with" the ground squirrels. Nobody had any illusions about what that meant, as capturing the squirrels live was out of the question because of the expense. Only one pest-control company in town had a license for squirrels, and they were restricted to live-trapping and relocating them, at $100 an hour. Mr. Douglas said he didn't care about the money, but the other HOA members, including Max, balked. The bills would rack up fast, and what if after several hundred dollars in payments, there was only a negligible reduction in the number of squirrels? Someone suggested poisoning them as a cheap alternative, but Eileen and others were concerned about the effect the poison might have on animals up the food chain. Among other things, the neighborhood had a resident family of Harris' hawks. Therefore, if even one of them were inadvertently killed, no one, least of all Eileen, would be able to forgive themselves.

As so often happens in deliberations by committee, the HOA's discussions ended in indecision. Max was left simply to "explore other options" and to report back at the next official HOA meeting in two months' time. But he had no intention of standing idly by, while the squirrels wreaked havoc. The state of Mr. Douglas' driveway had been a deciding factor. It was one thing, Max thought, for someone else's property to be destroyed; it was quite another for it to happen to his. For days, after seeing the damage inflicted by the squirrels, apocalyptic visions rose up in his mind: his yard becoming a veritable Gaza Strip of tunnels, his own driveway collapsing. He'd even heard—from where, he couldn't remember—of ground squirrels tunneling under garages and ruining foundations (it wasn't so farfetched — he'd heard of crazier things happening). That was all he needed. It would mean thousands of dollars in repairs.

To avoid this, he started patrolling his yard every morning for signs of squirrels. All he ever found were what appeared to be rat holes, but he didn't take any chances. With a shovel he cleared away the gravel and dug up and buried the runways and underground trenches for as far as he could unearth them. After a week of frenzied digging, his yard looked as if it had been worked over, haphazardly, by a plow. There had to be a better way.

Then an idea came to him. It was so simple it was ingenious; he'd buy one of those scoped air rifles and hunt the squirrels down. He called Arizona Game and Fish to find out whether it was legal to fire a pellet gun within the city limits. The only restriction was that air rifles couldn't exceed 0.30 caliber, which made the issue moot because most were barely half that size. He saw this as a green light to proceed. That very afternoon he went online and bought a Crosman TR77, a 250-count container of "Destroyer" pellets, and a gun case. During and after the purchase, he could hardly contain his excitement. He felt like a child awaiting the arrival of a new toy.

Coincidentally, Mr. Douglas had the same thought about shooting the squirrels. The day after the Crosman had been ordered, he sent an e-mail to Eileen (she was co-president of the HOA along with Mrs. Parks) suggesting half-seriously, half-facetiously that he and Max buy scoped air rifles and start sniping the squirrels. Eileen showed Max the e-mail, unaware a rifle was already on its way. "What do you think?" she asked dubiously—the thought of Mr. Douglas and her husband toting rifles around the neighborhood made her mildly squeamish. "Shall we at least consider it? We seem to be running out of options."

Max pretended it was the first he'd considered such a thing. In the clear light of day, now that the novelty of buying the gun had worn off, he was embarrassed at having come up with the idea himself. How exactly he'd intended to explain the postal delivery of a Crosman was unclear, but the fortuitous e-mail from Mr. Douglas gave him a way out. "I don't know," Max said in response to Eileen's question, feigning misgiving about the use of a gun. "Although ..." He was silent for a moment, as if deep in thought. "... maybe it *isn't* such a bad idea."

The package with the Crosman arrived a few days later. Max carried it into the living room and removed the packaging. He found the gun surprisingly heavy, weighing as it did more than six pounds, but its sophistication compensated for its weight. He held it up into the light: black from stock to muzzle, it was so menacing-looking it could have passed as a police tactical rifle. He felt a tingling sensation in his spine as he mounted the scope and lined up the crosshairs on nothing in particular out a window. *It'll do nicely*, he thought. In fact, it was all but a certainty now, with a rifle in hand, that the squirrels were doomed. He never did anything in half measures.

If it was a war the squirrels wanted, it was a war they were going to get.

Outside, not five minutes later, he spotted a squirrel munching a mesquite pod with impunity in front of the Sandbergs' house, catty-corner from his own. He cocked the rifle's break barrel against his thigh, inserted a pellet into the breach, and like an actor in a western, swung the barrel back into place. The scope still hadn't been sighted in, but there wasn't time for such niceties. He crossed the street and sat on the curb near Mr. Douglas' driveway, within twenty yards of the offending squirrel. Before lining up the crosshairs, he scanned the street for any sign of the neighbors. No one was about. He breathed a sigh of relief, as he had no desire to explain what he was doing with a rifle. Meanwhile the squirrel hadn't budged; it went on eating the mesquite pod, completely indifferent to Max's presence. He put the crosshairs on the animal's head, released the safety, took a deep breath, and fired. A puff of dust rose up from the ground about six feet in front of the squirrel, followed by a loud thwack against the metal door of the Sandbergs' garage. The squirrel, unscathed, looked around in bewilderment for a second and then darted into its burrow.

"Damn it," Max muttered and drew back the safety. Shaking his head, he propped the barrel of the gun onto his shoulder. The only consolation, he thought, was that no one from the neighborhood had heard the ricocheting pellet. Shamefacedly he stood up from the curb. Then he, too, scurried into his house to hide.

*

He was sure something had been with the rifle's scope; he'd never shot so poorly before. True, every gun had a break-in period, but falling six feet short of the target was ridiculous by any measure. So the next day, he set about zeroing the scope. After drawing a makeshift target on a piece of printer paper, he stapled it to a wooden stake, which he drove into the ground in the wash near his house. It was midday and suffocatingly hot. Other than the traffic on Fort Lowell Road and the occasional squeaky trill of a Gila woodpecker, the only sound was that of the cicadas, their songs a distinctively metallic drone in the dry desert heat. He squatted down a few yards from the target in the shade of a mesquite tree. He had a look of deadly earnest on his face. Tilting his bush hat farther back on his head, he drew up the rifle, centered the scope on the bull's eye, and fired. From where he was kneeling, he could see that the pellet had just clipped the outer ring on the bottom-right corner of the target. He'd been correct that the scope was off. No wonder he'd missed the squirrel so miserably the day before. There was no time to waste in fixing the problem. He removed the caps from the elevation and windage dials and, with a flat-edge screwdriver, turned each wheel two clicks up and to the left, respectively. He test fired again, and still the pellet struck more than three inches below and to the right of the center of the target. Several more times he adjusted the wheels until at last the scope was zeroed.

The moment he emerged from the wash, he saw two ground squirrels in Mr. Douglas' driveway: one near the curb, the other near the garage. Like the squirrel the day before, these two were indifferent to Max's presence, continuing to forage for mesquite pods even as he sat down on the curb, yards from Mr. Douglas' driveway. The squirrels became wary of him only after he'd shouldered his rifle. Suddenly the one near the curb scampered to the safety of its burrow but just as quickly returned to the surface, its head sticking up slightly above the dirt mound, as cautiously alert as a sentry. Max seized the opportunity: he centered the crosshairs on the squirrel's head and pulled the trigger. Instantly the squirrel fell to the ground, flopping spasmodically, like a convulsive break dancer. The death throes lasted another minute, and all the while Max kept thinking, *Why can't the damned thing die and be done with it?* It all seemed so over the top. When, finally, there was no longer any movement near the burrow, he went to check on the kill. The mound was spattered with blood, but the squirrel itself was nowhere to be seen. It couldn't possibly have survived a close-range shot to the head, so where was it? Dead in its burrow? That had to be the case. He would have noticed if it had run off.

As Max ruminated, the other squirrel watched him with an apparent mixture of curiosity and fear. Its head and eyes were just visible from a hole beneath one of the paving stones in Mr. Douglas' driveway. Remaining standing, Max reloaded his gun and took a few measured steps to his right to get a better vantage point. The squirrel didn't move, its eyes trained on him, suspiciously. He was presented with a perfect, straight-on shot. Without hesitating, he aimed the rifle and fired. The squirrel drew back an inch, convulsed a second, then collapsed under its own weight. *Thank God*, Max thought. *A clean shot.*

The image of the last squirrel, its body flailing about, still lingered uncomfortably in his mind, and he was feeling a prick of conscience about it. No animal, not even a pest, deserved unnecessary pain. He wanted the squirrels removed from the neighborhood, but not if it meant torturing them. He was almost ready to throw in the towel when it occurred to him that he had no choice in the matter. He had a job to perform. He and the other HOA members had already considered the alternatives, which were too expensive or equally grim. And doing nothing wasn't an option, either. If he were to leave the squirrels to their own devices, they'd destroy *his* driveway next, and *that* he couldn't allow. Which, of course, would mean more killing, something he was loath to do. But again, what choice did he have?

He leaned forward and, like a soldier planting a flag, drove the butt of his rifle into the ground. His situation was untenable. He was damned if he did and damned if he didn't. It was fortunate that he had a gun in his hands. He could take out his anger on some unsuspecting rodent, like the squirrel that happened to be relaxing under a fairy duster at the corner of the Dodds' garage, across the street and a good twenty yards from where he now stood. It was a tough shot, with foliage obstructing his view, but he was feeling infallible. He loaded his rifle and fired before he knew what he was doing. There was the sound of breaking branches and metal on rock, after which the squirrel stutter-stepped out from under the shrub, cowering its way, inch by inch, into an escape hole, where it disappeared. Max went to the hole. On its outer edge was a single spot of blood, no bigger than a pinkie nail. The squirrel must have only been nicked. Somehow this made Max's ire dissipate—firing the rifle without killing anything apparently acting as a release—and as a result he was ready to call it quits. He'd had enough carnage for one day.

*

Late the following morning, he was getting into his car to drive to the grocery store when he noticed two more ground squirrels. One of them was resting on its haunches in the middle of the Sandbergs' driveway, nonchalantly sunning itself and surveying its surroundings. The other one was foraging closer to the house. "The little bastards," Max said aloud, echoing Mr. Douglas' moniker. He slammed shut his car door and stood staring at the devious rodents with hatred in his eyes. How could there be so many of the damned things? They were everywhere. The shopping, he supposed, would have to wait. He hadn't intended to hunt today, but clearly he hadn't realized the direness of the situation. There had to be a whole colony of squirrels in the neighborhood, and the thought of even one of them tunneling under his driveway made him shudder. He would have to act swiftly, and with shock and awe, or else he might never be able to keep the animals in check.

Two minutes later he found himself sitting on the curb across the street from the Sandbergs', his rifle pointing at the squirrel in the driveway. Despite his recent shooting, neither of the squirrels had become gunwise; they went about their business as if nothing were amiss. He fired. At first the squirrel stood stock-still, but then slowly, its feet remaining firmly planted on the ground, it tilted forward, like a tree being felled. It hit the pavers with its body spread full length. Max assumed it was dead on impact, but shortly afterward it stirred to life. (By this point the other squirrel had vanished.) Zombie-like, it slowly and shakily lifted its upper torso and dragged itself toward a Cordia shrub at the edge of the driveway. Centimeter by centimeter it struggled, a faint streak of blood in its wake. On reaching the shrub, it heaved itself onto a lower branch, hung there precariously for an instant, and then flopped down to the ground. Freakishly it clung to life. Max looked on in horror as it did a one-eighty and headed back up the driveway. He would have shot it a second time to put it out of its misery, but he was seized by a sudden paralysis of will. For an uncomfortably long time, the squirrel crawled with what little strength it had left to the Sandbergs' backyard, where, Max was certain, a slow and agonizing death awaited it.

*

Only after reading *National Geographic* a week later, did he have the courage to hunt again. There was an article about elephants encroaching on African villages that were being culled to reduce conflict with humans. Apparently for the culling to be effective in a given locale, the kill rate had to be at least seventy percent; otherwise the animals would come back with a vengeance because of the increased availability of food. It occurred to Max, as he read the article, that the same might be true of the ground squirrels in his neighborhood. To date, he was lucky if he'd killed twenty percent of them, and if he did nothing further, in a couple of months, there might be more than when he'd started. It was a disturbing thought—and one he couldn't abide. He resolved to reach the seventy-percent cull target and at the same time avoid a repeat of his last outing. He spent the better part of a Friday afternoon re-sighting the scope of his rifle. A sheet of pellet-riddled printer paper later, he set out to hunt.

The reception he got was unexpected. From his front stoop he heard a high-pitched whistle, and in a flash the handful of squirrels above ground scattered to their respective holes. Somehow during the last week they'd become skittish. He'd have to up his game if he was going to shoot them now. For a start, he'd have to be more patient. He knew that that was something *he* could afford but the squirrels could not; sooner or later they'd have to come out of their holes if they wanted food. And anyway, it never paid to hurry your shot. Either you missed your quarry entirely, or worse, you … but before he could finish his thought, the image of the squirrel with the broken spine crept like a wounded animal into his mind. *Oh, God.* If patience was what he needed to avoid *that,* then so be it. Mustering what patience he could, he sat down on the curb in the shade of a mesquite tree and waited. He didn't have to wait long. The squirrels' heads began to pop up from their holes one by one, like in a carnival shooter game, until several pairs of tiny eyes were warily fixed on him.

It was then the real carnage began. He started with the squirrel directly across the street. Through the scope of his rifle, he could see the top of its head poking out from a hole beneath one of the Dodds' birds of paradise. His heart pounded as he flipped the safety. He took a deep breath, slowly exhaled. The pellet hit the squirrel right between the eyes. It twitched momentarily at the mouth of the hole before expiring. Scarcely had it done so than Max saw another squirrel rise up from a hole by a saguaro off the Wrights' garage. It stood fully upright, looking at him as if it were curious to know what had just happened. This time the force of the pellet was so great it went clean through the squirrel's skull, smacking the saguaro behind it. As its body flung backward and jammed, head first, into an adjacent hole, Max's rifle moved as if of its own accord and sighted in a third squirrel. Soon it, too, was dead. It lay near the Sandbergs' driveway, its back wedged between two water-meter plates, all four paws pointing absurdly straight up toward the sky.

So much for patience.

There was no stopping Max now. He felt a rush of adrenaline as he glimpsed a fourth squirrel skulking between the Dodds' and the Wrights' garages. He drew a bead on it, but before he could fire, it disappeared into a fifteen-foot length of plastic tubing that had been left out for bulk-garbage pickup. He set down his gun and hurried to the tube. He had to prevent the squirrel from escaping out the other end. He made quick work of lifting the tube and forming it into a ring. The squirrel's claws scraped along the plastic as it slid to the ring's center. Still holding the tubing in his hands, Max went to the Dodds' garbage bin and with an index finger pried open the lid. Then he dropped both ends of the tube into the bin and began shaking it frantically. Something deep within him, a primeval blood lust, compelled him forward. Harder and harder he shook the tube. Eventually the squirrel thumped out, landing on a bed of leaf litter at the bottom of the bin. Helpless and quivering, it looked up at Max in a way that seemed imploring. But Max wasn't fazed; he'd become numb to violence. Without thinking twice he retrieved the gun and shot the squirrel point blank. It squirmed, then went limp and oozed down through a gap in the leaves, a droplet of blood the only sign of what had been there before. Max closed the bin, stepped back, and looked triumphantly out over the neighborhood, the common areas now a seeming wasteland of rotting squirrel carcasses.

*

The sudden absence of ground squirrels hadn't gone unnoticed. The next afternoon Mrs. Parks accosted Max as he pulled his car into his garage. Reluctantly, he put down the driver's side window. She shuffled toward the car, her flip-flops slapping the soles of her feet with each hurried step. Leaning through the open window, inches from his face, she said breathlessly, "You have to *do* something."

He drew away from her. "Do something about what?"

"About the rat," she said. She looked in the direction of a furry lump lying near the Sandbergs' driveway. Her dog Freddie, it seemed, had found a dead rat on the road and had eaten part of it before she could prevent him. "It's the biggest, most god-awful rat I've ever seen, and I don't have the stomach to clean it up myself. Would you mind doing it?" She gave Max a knowing look. "You seem to be good at that kind of thing."

He told her he would, both out of curiosity and to get rid of her. But what he found after they'd parted wasn't a rat. It was one of the ground squirrels he'd shot the previous day. Freddie must have dragged it from between the water-meter plates. He understood why Mrs. Parks hadn't had the stomach to remove it, as he hardly did himself. Out in the open the smell was only faintly putrid, like a piece of meat in the early stages of decay, but the state of the squirrel's corpse was nothing short of grotesque. The sun had bloated it to nearly twice its original size, and Max could have sworn, when he kneeled down to get a better look at it, that he saw something move near its tail. *Maggots of a house fly? Could they really propagate overnight?* Luckily, it was garbage pick-up day, and the Sandbergs' garbage bin was only a few feet away. He retrieved a shovel, scooped up the gaseous monstrosity with a modicum of effort, and dropped it into the bin. That was the last, he hoped, he'd have to deal with ground squirrels again for a while.

*

As it turned out, it *was* the last he had to deal with ground squirrels, at least until the following year; it just wasn't the last he had to deal with rodents. A vacuum had been created by the decimation of the squirrels, and something more pernicious began to take their place. Three weeks after the incident with Freddie, Mrs. Parks came running to Max's front door early in the morning. She was still wearing her nightdress, her hair disheveled, dark patches under her eyes, appearing sleep deprived. "Rats again," she said, nearly hyperventilating. He hadn't told her that the "rat" Freddie had found, had actually been a squirrel; it would have raised uncomfortable questions. "I think they've gnawed through the engine of my car," she continued. "I can't get it started. And I found bits of wire and hose on the ground by the front tires."

By rats, he presumed, she meant packrats. To his mind they weren't quite as nasty as brown rats, which roamed the sewers. Packrats seemed more hygienic because they nested in wood piles or under the thorny protection of prickly pear. Even so, he despised them. He'd seen one, once, at the crack of dawn while he was on a walk. It came creeping out of a drainage pipe, its long, bushy tail trailing disgustingly behind it. His stomach churned at the thought. The last thing he wanted was an animal like that sneaking around his garage. "I'll do what I can," he said, deliberately tempering his enthusiasm in front of Mrs. Parks, for he knew combating packrats wouldn't be easy.

They were a tricky bunch, to be sure. Unlike ground squirrels, rats were nocturnal — and wilier. You couldn't shoot them, and they could easily outsmart the average trap. Poison was probably the best route. A little cyanide, perhaps. Or an anticoagulant. He was aware of one, for example, under the chemical name brodifacoum, a rodenticide that apparently worked wonders by making the animals bleed to death internally. Not a happy thought, but then what was the alternative? Something worse, that was what. Already he saw in his mind's eye what he'd do: he'd strategically place around the neighborhood peanut-butter crackers laced with Rodenthor, although before he could proceed, he'd have to convince Eileen and the neighbors of the merits of chemical warfare, which would be a hard sell. Collateral damage and all that. He might be better off going rogue and keeping them in the dark. Either way, he could see that a solution to the problem was a long way off. In fact it appeared the war against rodents had only just begun.

Author's Bio:

Jason Zeitler is the author of the novella Like Flesh to the Scalpel. His short stories and narrative essays have appeared in Midwestern Gothic and in other print and online magazines. He lives in Tucson with his wife and son.

The One that Got Away

By Gemma L. Brook

"How about you, George? What's your best lure-and-lost story?"

Attention turned to the middle one of the group. He put down his mug and wiped the foam from his beard. "You sure you want to hear it?"

Affirmation chorused around the table and drowned out the commotion in the tavern. George raised a hand in acquiescence. "All right, all right," he said. He took a long draft from his dark ale, then waved to the waitress. "Another round for the table."

"You're stalling," red-haired Abe accused with a grin.

"Am not," George replied with calm, as a waitress filled their mugs.

"It was a dark and stormy night!" mocked his cronies.

"Was not," George insisted, glaring at them from beneath his brambly grey brows. "Dark, but clear and calm. Stars shone off the water like a mermaid's mirror. All I could see was the ripples the beast made as it passed beneath the surface, shadow under shadow." His hand undulated over the table. The laughter died down. "Bigger than this table it was, long and lean."

Abe and Murray exchanged knowing smiles. "So what'd you bait it with?" Murray asked. "A foot long bass?"

George gave Murray a look of pity. "With gold," he said.

Ivan snorted. "Where'd you get gold?"

George caught his eye. "From my wife's jewelry box."

Another round of laughter. "Oh, bet she was happy with that," Murray said.

"'Specially when you came home empty-handed!" Abe added.

George cocked a brow. "Never said I came home empty-handed."

That got their attention. Ivan pretended to clean under his nails with his knife, but everyone's eyes were on George. "So...?" Ivan prompted.

George leaned back in his chair. "It was her anniversary necklace," he said. "Double-long gold chain. I made a loop of it, and a float of a champagne cork."

"Fitting," Ivan said with a nod.

"Dallied it over the water," George went on, "trailing it back and forth just so." His hand made a sinuous motion as it hovered over the polished tabletop. "I could see the beast moving under the surface, circling under that ring of gold. Eying it." He watched the other men. "I kept it moving, slow and easy, but with a death grip on the end. I could see the beast's eyes, gleaming like emeralds, for just one second. Then its head shot up to grab the chain, but I pulled it tight around its neck, and I had it! It came out of the water, thrashing all green and gold, tossing its mane, pawing the water into foam with its pearly hooves. Most beautiful thing I ever seen...and the most wild."

Abe's mouth was wide. So were Murray's eyes. Even Ivan was riveted. "What happened next?" they asked.

George shook his head, looking from one to the other. "You wouldn't believe it." At their angry protest, he held up his hand. "But I'll tell you anyway." He leaned forward on his elbows, as did they. "It changed, right before my eyes. Shrank as thin as an eel and slithered right out of my chain bridle. Then it dove like a porpoise and vanished. And the water closed over it without a ripple, like it'd never been there."

They all thumped back into their chairs. Ivan grinned through his beard. "Good one George. I'll buy the next round just for that." The group laughed in agreement.

"But you said you weren't empty-handed," Abe reminded him.

George smiled a broad, slow smile, as he reached into his vest pocket and pulled out a long chain of gold. He spread it out on the table before them.

"At least you got your wife's chain back," Murray said with a wink.

George just kept on smiling. "And more. Look closer."

They all leaned in. Their brows creased with curiosity as they studied it, then their eyes went wide. Caught in the links were strands of mane, fine as silk and green as emeralds. "Wife likes it even better now," George said, before he gathered it carefully up into his hand and slipped it into his pocket again.

Author's Bio:

Gemma L. Brook was raised with the love of stories. Her mother was an ardent bibliophile and her father a delightful raconteur. Her three wonderfully different and creative sisters nurtured her imagination and curiosity. Mythology, folklore, and legends have fascinated her from a tender age; later, comic books and science fiction added to those interests. By fifth grade she was writing her own stories and determined to become a published author. In college, she followed her dreams and studied myth and classical literature.

Decades of writing later, a career change encouraged by her supportive husband enabled her to pursue her passion more seriously, and she joined Pennwriters, Inc. and two critique groups. The talented writers of those three groups have inspired and supported her quest to become an ever-evolving and improving author, still delving into the realms of myth and legend. You can find and connect with Gemma on her website, gemmabrookwriter.com

Monkey in the Middle

By Audra Supplee

Their week at the cabin on Silverset Lake, Maine was supposed to be awesome. Even though the lake was deep in the woods and even though eight-year-old Nickie would be the only kid, it still held possibilities. First of all, Daddy agreed to join Nickie and her mom, making them a family again, if only for one week. He even rented a boat. And *then*, just as they were sitting down to lunch, Uncle Victor, Nickie's most favorite grownup in the whole world, drove up the gravel lane.

"Just passing through." He pulled a duffle bag from the trunk of his rental. "Don't mind if I crash for a few nights do you?"

Mom smiled. "The more the merrier." She also mumbled, "What a surprise," in a voice that didn't sound merry or surprised.

"Long time, no see," Daddy said, which was a joke 'cause they had just finished a world tour two days ago.

Nickie galloped into Uncle Victor's open arms. Best of all, he gave her a pair of shiny blue drumsticks.

The trouble started soon after she knelt on the floor and started drumming on the cabin's lumpy sofa cushions. That was when she noticed the angry whispers. As she joyfully beat up a dust cloud, Mom and Daddy hissed at each other from the kitchen area. Later, Daddy muttered through clenched teeth at Victor.

By the time they climbed aboard Daddy's boat to ride to dinner later, the grownups had stopped talking altogether. Nickie sat in the back beside a glowering Victor. Her mom sat up front, arms folded across her middle, tight as a clenched fist.

The boat's twin engines grumbled to life. Daddy jammed the throttle forward with a jerk. Nickie's back slammed against the cushioned seat. She giggled at the sudden burst of speed, couldn't help herself, even with trouble brewing.

They sliced through water smooth as a window, raced beside a green blur that didn't turn back into the surrounding pine forest, until Daddy gave in to the Tasmanian Devil sound of Mom's voice. "Slow down, for the love of God!"

It was Daddy's idea to cross the lake to the restaurant in their boat. He promised steamed clams and candles on the tables and giant windows overlooking the water. He promised a perfect night out for everybody, except…

Mom said she didn't want to go. Victor growled that he'd rather stay behind. Then Daddy said in his King voice, "Either we're all going or nobody goes."

Nickie believed him. She fell at his feet and whined that she never got to do anything fun.

The fact that they made it to the restaurant's wooden pier, came as a happy surprise.

Once inside, they followed a lady who cradled three large menus for the grownups and a shiny menu with a smiling cartoon fish for Nickie. They passed a lobster tank, and the aroma of melted butter and fish from the kitchen. They passed a dark paneled lounge from which billowed cigarette smoke. They finally entered the sunny main dining room, where a wall of windows overlooked the lake. It was perfect, just like Daddy promised, except…

Mom flounced ahead with her flowery skirt swaying. Daddy,

dressed in a navy knit shirt and white jeans, stalked behind her, eyes straight ahead. Nickie slipped between them, but neither seemed to notice. She peered over her shoulder at Uncle Victor. He looked like a school teacher in a short-sleeved white shirt and purple striped necktie. He didn't smile back. He was watching a busboy bent over an empty table, scooping coins from the ashtray.

Nickie faced forward again. She wanted a table by the big window, so she could watch their boat. They were early enough so that most of the window booths were vacant, except...

The lady put their menus on a table in the center of the room instead. Nickie puffed in annoyance and slid into her chair. While the others took their places around the condiment cluttered table, Nickie peered under her paper placemat to see if there were any puzzles on the back side. Nothing. She slumped forward with a sigh.

"Elbows," Mom said from across the table.

Nickie sat up. A familiar scent spiked the air and caught her attention. She recognized it as her daddy's fresh, sweet cologne. When she leaned toward Uncle Victor, who sat across from Daddy, she smelled the same familiar scent on him too.

Victor wasn't really her uncle. He played drums in Daddy's band. On days off from school, when her mom let her, Nickie joined Daddy on tour. Nickie got to spend fun times with Victor because he was Daddy's roommate, when the band traveled. Secretly Mom called him, "Daddy's little friend." Whenever Mom said that, Nickie had to laugh. Victor stood head and shoulders above Daddy.

Nickie bobbed from left to right, sniffing their identical cologne. "I'm smelling in stereo," she announced.

"I'd rather you didn't," Daddy said.

Nickie tucked her linen napkin into the V-neck of her soccer shirt. Mom wanted her to wear a dress tonight, but Daddy let her wear her soccer uniform. That was one of the advantages to having parents about to split up. Nickie was bound to find at least one who was willing to let her have her way.

"Honey, the napkin goes on your lap," Mom said.

"What if I want lobster?" she asked.

"You don't."

Nickie slapped the napkin on her bare knees. This was not going to be a fun dinner, she could tell already.

A smiling waitress placed water glasses in front of each of them. "Our soups tonight are New England clam chowder and French onion."

Uncle Victor leaned toward Nickie. A lock of raven hair fell across his pale forehead. He whispered, "Would mademoiselle care for zee zoop wiz ze Frenchy onions or zee zoop wiz zee clammy chow?"

Nickie giggled. Daddy cleared his throat and gave them a sharp look.

The waitress asked for their drink order.

Nickie shot her arm up into the air, just like at school. "Coke, please!"

"White milk or chocolate," Mom corrected her.

The waitress made a sad face. "I'm sorry. We're out of chocolate milk tonight."

Nickie knew exactly how to make it work. "Ya got hot fudge sundaes?"

"You're not having a hot fudge sundae for dinner," Daddy said.

Nickie let out an exasperated sigh. "I know that. But if you mix the fudge in the milk you'll get—"

"She'll have plain white milk," Daddy told the waitress.

Nickie folded her arms and huffed. What was the matter with him today? He used to be fun at restaurants. Didn't he remember the time they flicked peas at Uncle Victor?

The waitress left to collect their drinks. Victor gently tapped on the gray table cloth. He alternated fingertips; right-left-right-right-left-right-left-left. Paradiddles. He had taught Nickie how to play them ages ago.

Nickie nodded to the rhythm and lightly fingered the multicolored bracelet on her left wrist. She made it for her afternoon project. Hoping to cheer up the grownups, she had carefully slipped tiny beads onto black thread until she had created four bracelets with special colors for each of them. She used pink and white for Mom to remind her she was pretty, even if she did think she was getting fat. She picked loud colors for Uncle Victor: purple and bright green. She hadn't planned it, but the bracelet dangling from his slender wrist matched the purple in his necktie. Daddy's blue and black bracelet would have matched his shirt, too. Nobody could see it though. Before they had left home, Nickie watched as he tucked it under his gold watchband. If she looked hard enough, she could spot one of the blue beads poking out of its hiding place.

She lifted her gaze to Daddy's heart-shaped face, shiny and red from too much sun. His eyes were closed, thin lips pressed tightly together. Headache, Nickie guessed. Hoping to make him smile, she plucked two round oyster crackers from the bowl next to the Tabasco sauce. She popped them into her cheeks. "Ook! Ahma ip-unk."

Daddy's long lashed eyes sprang open. "Chew it," he ordered.

That wasn't the reaction she'd hoped for, but she complied. Her right molars crunched down on one of the crackers. There wasn't enough room in her mouth for the other. A gooey ball plopped onto her laminated menu.

"Nickie!" Mom whispered harshly.

"You're supposed to eat those things, not play with them." Daddy snatched up the wet blob and dropped it in the empty ashtray. He wiped his hand on his napkin, his blue-gray eyes bored through her the whole time. Nickie looked away. She pretended to check her silverware for spots.

A minute later Mom loved her again and said in a friendly voice, "Sweetie, before the waitress gets back, do you want chicken fingers tonight or fried shrimp?"

Nickie grinned at the only person who hadn't yelled at her yet. "I want the same as Uncle Victor."

His blue eyes glistened with mischief. "What if I order steamed squid over rice?"

She fell against the back of her chair and laughed. Who would order a squishy squid with all those legs? No, they weren't called legs. "Don't squids have testicles like octopuses?"

She knew she got the word wrong when Daddy slapped his forehead.

"Honey, I think you mean *tentacles*," Mom said in an understanding tone.

"She knows what they're called."

"I forgot! I can't remember everything."

"Settle down." He turned to Mom, all smiles. "Why don't we order the Captain's Sampler? Remember when we used to get that?"

"I feel like dinner for one tonight. Why don't you and Victor share?"

"No. I believe he's having testicles over rice."

"They're called *tentacles*," Nickie said, now that she knew.

"I'm not allowed to have that anymore apparently," Victor snapped back.

The waitress reappeared with a smile and a tray of drinks. All the grownups stiffened.

"Ready to order?"

"Could we have another minute, please?" Daddy used his Prince Charming voice. "I can't decide."

"What a surprise," Victor and Mom said in unison.

They grinned and slapped a high-five.

After the waitress left, Daddy ducked behind his menu. "I don't know any of you people."

Mom crossed her eyes at him, but he missed it. Uncle Victor pushed up his nose to make a pig face. Daddy missed that, too. Nickie grinned and played along by sticking out her tongue. He didn't see that either.

"So what's it gonna be, big boy?" Mom teased. "Tuna or tentacles?"

Dad lowered his menu and gave her an icy stare.

"It's gotta be the tuna," Victor snapped back. "We all know he prefers the charade that his tentacles are only to be admired from afar."

"Everybody listen." Nickie spread her arms wide, "Nobody orders the squid. All right? Nobody gets it."

"You got that right," Victor muttered.

Mom snorted into her hand.

"That's ruddy hilarious, that is," Dad said, still glaring.

"If I didn't laugh ..." Mom's eyes turned shiny like she might cry. She took a sip of her wine instead.

"I'm not laughing," Nickie piped up. "Know why? 'Cause you guys aren't funny."

Uncle Victor tweaked one of her ponytails. "You are so right, Peanut. There's nothing funny going on."

Daddy frowned at Victor. "This isn't the time."

"It never *is*."

"Guys," Mom barked. "We're having a nice night out."

Nickie reached for the bread sticks. Maybe if she shoved a couple up her nose and said she was a walrus Daddy and Uncle Victor would stop staring at each other with the eye-daggers-of-death.

"Don't you dare start drumming with those," Mom said.

Daddy beckoned her with his index finger. Nickie leaned toward his end of the table.

"Do you want a spanking?"

She gasped and bolted upright. Mom made the punishment rules and they were timeouts.

"Then just sit there," Daddy ordered.

Nickie glared at the unlit candle in the middle of the table. What happened to the fun daddy, the one who used to have pillow fights with her in their hotel room? Where was the daddy who let her eat popcorn in bed and told monster stories in sign language when he had to rest his singing voice? That daddy laughed all the time. He even cracked up over room mix-ups, like the time on tour when there was only one king-sized bed in their room. They had piled in together, Daddy on her left and Uncle Victor on her right. Victor had called Nickie the monkey- in-the-middle and they all laughed. Daddy added, "I hope the *monkey* can keep a secret." He and Victor laughed even harder, so Nickie did too.

When the waitress came back for their order, Nickie used her *good girl* voice. "Fried shrimp, please," but Daddy wasn't paying attention. He was too busy asking the waitress to bring him another drink when she got the chance.

After the waitress whisked away, Mom turned to Victor. "Stick with the ice tea, you're the designated driver."

"I'm not getting drunk," Daddy snarled.

Nickie frowned at him. "You need a nap."

"Do you want to step outside with me?" he asked.

"No thank you." Nickie bit into a bread stick.

"Give the poor kid a break," said Victor. "She's not doing anything."

"You're a child expert all of a sudden I suppose." Daddy wasn't having it.

"If the both of you don't stop it, I'm leaving," Mom said. "And I don't care if I have to swim across the lake to get away from both of you all.."

Nickie fidgeted. If this kept up they all might go home without dinner. Her napkin slid off her lap, giving her an excuse to escape under the table. It felt cozy down there, weaving between Daddy's high-tops, Mom's sandals and Victor's loafers. Best of all, feet didn't frown.

Something shiny in the maroon carpeting by Mom's heel caught her eye. Nickie had just reached for it when the rubber tip of Daddy's shoe nudged her in the haunch. She snatched the coin and peeked out from under the table.

"Look!" She held it up. "I found a quarter."

Daddy clasped her wrist and tugged her to her feet. "That's it."

He pulled her away from the table and toward a side door. Nickie dug her sneakers into the carpet, hoping to slow him down long enough to remember he wasn't allowed to hit her. Daddy yanked her away from Mom, away from Uncle Victor and out of the restaurant to a wooden bench facing the lake. He pointed at the bench, until she reluctantly dropped onto it.

"What's the matter with you tonight?" he demanded.

"I didn't tell my napkin to fall. It was an accident."

"You didn't have to crawl under the table after it. You're too old for that."

She pushed out her bottom lip and bowed her head.

"When we go back inside ..."

Her head snapped up. "I'm not going back. Everybody hates each other in there."

Daddy inhaled deeply and let the air out in a long sigh. "That's not exactly true." He sank into the bench next to her. "We're all a bit on edge, but we still care about each other."

"Nobody's acting like it."

He kissed the top of her head. "We'll try harder."

"All day long everybody keeps telling me, 'go brush your teeth,

Nickie, go wash your hands,' even when I don't have to, just so you guys can have secrets without me. How come nobody tells me secret things?"

He put his arm around her. "All right," he said softly. "We'll have a secret talk."

Nickie frowned. Her throat still wanted to argue. After allowing a moment for the suggestion to sink in she said, "Okay. Tell me a secret."

He leaned close so his face was level with hers. "Sometimes," he whispered, "for no reason whatever, my hand does this."

He opened and closed his fist, over and over, then moved his pulsing hand toward her and tickled her ribs.

Nickie didn't want to giggle, but couldn't help it. She jabbed him with her elbow. They weren't supposed to be laughing now. Private talks were serious.

Daddy sat back with his arms folded. "You know I love you. We all do. It's the love between the rest of us we're having trouble sorting out."

The setting sun reflected off the water, turning parts of the lake bright orange. Nickie gazed at the dazzling water. It was quiet here, no cars, no city lights, just calm water and pine trees, the wharf and Daddy's boat.

"This vacation will probably be the last time we'll be together as a family." After a long silence he added, "Mummy explained that to you, right?"

Nickie only shrugged. She understood divorce. Some of her classmates had dual homes after all. Besides, Daddy's tours kept the family apart so much it almost felt like they were already divorced.

She reached for his hand. His long fingers lightly closed around hers. With her free hand, she gave his watchband a tug and released the hidden bracelet. Nickie tapped her finger over the beads. Blue,

blue, black, blue, blue, black, all the way around, except the one place where she accidentally dropped three blues in a row, but hadn't noticed till she had finished.

She peered up. "Don't you like it?"

"Of course I do. You made it. Men don't usually wear this kind of jewelry though."

"Uncle Victor does."

"Well … he's different."

Nickie knew Victor was different. That's what made him special. Victor hadn't changed and yet she felt something had gone wrong between him and her dad. The last time she toured with them they had laughed all the time, even over silly stuff like painting chocolate pudding mustaches on each other or tossing water balloons at the other guys from the band. Ever since Victor showed up, Daddy acted grumpy. Victor wasn't a real uncle which probably meant he wouldn't get visitation if he and Dad divorced too.

"Uncle Victor isn't just your friend," Nickie said.

"That's all he is, I swear it," Daddy blurted.

"Nuh uh! He's my friend, too."

"Oh." Daddy sat back, relieved. "Right."

"Maybe even more than a friend. Like another dad."

"Let's not go that far."

Nickie bowed her head. *Things will be different.* That's what her mom told her ages ago. Some things were already different. Daddy didn't come home as often and Mom had started going on dates with Nickie's art teacher.

Nickie breathed out a big sigh. "I don't want everything to change."

Daddy hunched forward, elbows on his knees. He stared at the lake for a long time. "I don't either, sunshine. Sometimes they do anyway."

"Does that mean we'll never laugh at dinner again?"

He glanced at her out of the corner of his eyes. "What would make you laugh at dinner?"

A devilish thought made Nickie grin. "Flying food is always funny."

Daddy sat up. "Mummy would never allow that. But, if we got some extra straws, she just might let us blow the papers at each other."

Satisfied, Nickie skipped back inside with her dad.

"Everything all right?" Mom asked.

Daddy gave her a thumbs-up. Before he took his seat, he motioned to the waitress. He grinned and held up a fist full of straws wrapped in white paper.

Mom smiled. "What are you going to do with all that?"

He winked at her and handed them out. "For old time's sake."

Within seconds skinny white papers flew from all directions. One landed in Mom's hair. Victor pretended one poked out his eye. Daddy held one above his mouth like a mustache and started talking in a funny accent. Nickie laughed so hard her belly ached. She loved all of them for being funny and perfect again, except…

It stopped as quickly as it had begun. Mom scurried to the ladies' room, sniffling. For a long time it was just the three of them, Daddy on her left and Victor on her right. She was the monkey in the middle again. This time nobody was laughing and Nickie wasn't sure why.

Author's Bio:

Aud Supplee, an expert child (and has been one for well-over 40 years), has two published novels for middle grade readers. The first, *Standing Ovation*, published under her maiden name by a New York publisher, is sadly out of print. The second, *I Almost Love You, Eddie Clegg*, was published by Peachtree Publishers.

Even in her adult stories, children are featured, as are musicians. A music lover, Aud has played trumpet, drums, keyboards and electric guitar, but not all at once; that might get tricky. If she were to clone herself, she could form a really bad garage band. That is what inspired her to write about professional musicians rather than becoming one.

Her novella, *Broken Soul to Broken Soul* (a story surprisingly devoid of musicians, but not without kids), will be featured in an upcoming anthology also published by Running Wild Press.

You can visit her online at www.audsupplee.com where she blogs on the categories of Live, Read, Write, which sum up her creative process. She can also be found on Instagram (@audsupplee).

Note: No professional musicians were harmed during the creation of this story.

Le Bouquiniste

By Lorna Walsh

Anton Marchand deplores those who sell shiny souvenirs to survive. He has been known to declare he would rather be poor than a pedlar of plastic, so penniless is he. Beside the river, where the Bouquinistes have traded for centuries, he sits in a folding chair and puffs on thin cigarettes, as tourists peer into his green trunk of books. Whenever one is pulled from its row, Anton stiffens, as if it were one of his own vertebrae, and he braces himself for the inevitable.

"100 euro? But it's falling apart!"

Anton translates whatever language is spoken by the tone of voice, or facial expression, and bellows his retort in French, "A good book is more than the words on its pages. The story of the book *itself* is just as important. Think of the journey it has made, the hands it has passed through, the houses it has lived in!"

The tourists hear his fury and leave him muttering to himself. Imbeciles. They believe the value of a book diminishes, the more fragile it becomes, and the older Anton grows, the angrier he becomes. Over the years, he has lost interest in books with pristine pages and unbroken spines. Now he acquires, for sale, only the battered, the tattered, and the coffee spattered, in the belief that no matter how pitiful a book's condition, there must be *someone* out there who wants it.

One hot day in June, Anton hears the Americans. Their voices soar above the noise of traffic and the bells of Notre Dame de Paris. Anton reaches for a bottle beneath his chair, tips more red wine into a tumbler, and inwardly roils with disdain.

Soon there are eight of them, all braying over the oldest books and rubbing their fingers on the worn leather. Anton fumes at their covetousness, their desire to buy age from all over the world to take back to their pubescent country. After several pain-filled minutes, one of his most treasured tomes is chosen and, though excessively compensated, Anton slumps into his seat to grieve his loss, while the group is lured away by trinkets twinkling in the sunlight.

One, however, stays behind. The woman pushes up her sunglasses into her well-coiffed hair and bends forward to inspect the volumes. Her hair, nails, and teeth have all been colored by chemicals. Only the skin on her neck and hands indicate she might, in fact, be as old as Anton, who feels in his bones each and every year of his half century.

Anton eyes her breasts, which push against her tight, low-cut top. He looks away and then returns his gaze. They are round and smooth, like firm balls of bread dough, and clearly made to be looked at. In Anton's experience, when Americans spend money, they want you to appreciate it. But these breasts are too spherical. Anton prefers flatter breasts, like used pastry bags with just a little firmness left beneath large nozzles—the breasts of a woman whose life story includes a chapter on motherhood.

The American lifts out a book, cooing and purring over the exquisite jacket. She buries her nose between the pages, breathes in its age, and then turns to Anton. "My friends have no interest in literature," she says. Anton's eyebrows register his surprise on hearing perfect French. Smiling, she tells him, "I'm a high school French teacher in Louisiana. It's wonderful to speak the language properly again!"

Anton suppresses the urge to return the smile, because he knows it makes his face look strange. He concedes he may have been deceived by the woman's immaculate appearance and is reminded how easy it is to overlook a rare book if it has been re-bound and re-stitched. When he brushes off the ash that has dropped into his lap, he registers the fact he has hardened a little. He crosses his legs and tries to think about something else, but he is soon watching again.

The woman's hand moves lightly above a line of books, fingers twitching like divining rods. No wedding band, Anton notes. Then, sensing something, her hand hovers. She gives off a squeal of delight as she lifts out a children's book, so slim it had been almost invisible between two thick volumes.

"I know this book!" she says, addressing the illustration on the cover. A buck-toothed rabbit sitting in a magician's hat smiles back at her.

Anton nods distractedly, imagining the scars under her breasts left by the cosmetic surgeon. Anton wants to know why she had felt incomplete, if someone had made her feel that way, and whether her breasts bounce with happiness when she makes love, or if they feel heavy with the weight of regret.

"Oh my God!"

The woman's cry snaps Anton out of his reverie, and he jumps up from the chair—his once famous chivalric instinct returning for a split second. He stares at the woman, unable to interpret her look of distress. Drama is something Anton finds only in books, no longer in his humdrum life. The woman has turned pale.

"Please," he says, gesturing to his chair.

She drops into it, gulps down the wine offered to her and puts down the glass.

"May I have a cigarette?" she whispers.

Anton pulls the spare from behind his ear.

"Light it for me?" she asks.

He sucks the flame into the cigarette and puts it into her trembling hand. She takes deep inhalations, holds in the smoke for a long time, and then blows it out through her nose. After a minute, she passes the book to Anton. He flips through the pages. A first edition. Very charming illustrations, which must be the reason he acquired it.

"Read the inscription," she says.

He turns to the inside cover and reads aloud what is written in French: *"To my darling Bonnie, with love forever, from Grandmama."*

Anton looks at the woman and she stares back, eyes wide. He points at her, then to the book. "You are Bonnie? You are *this* Bonnie?"

The woman nods. "It's mine! The very same book I had as a child in Louisiana!" She begins to cry.

Anton shakes his head slowly. It cannot be possible. How can a book and its owner—separated by decades and continents—cross paths like this? It is, he thinks, the kind of coincidence that might flow from the quill of a great literary romantic onto the pages of a corpulent novel, but real life is not so wondrous. In his own life, at least, none of the treasures he has lost have ever been returned to him. No, this reunion cannot be pure chance. It must be that this woman, probably without knowing it, has always been searching for this one book, a token of a happier time long before the slice of a surgeon's knife: simply a matter of seek and ye shall find.

Yet Anton's heart is pumping, working hard to remind him that it used to beat for something other than the discovery of a rare book and that he was once a romantic, great in his own way. Perhaps, he thinks, the Fates had not been trying to unite Bonnie and the book, but to bring Bonnie to him.

During his speechlessness, Bonnie's tears have ceased, although she sniffs between sobs. Concerned passers-by dart disapproving looks at Anton. He pulls out his handkerchief, wishing he had a cleaner one. "You have had a great shock." Then, suddenly wanting to open her up and look inside, says in English, "Tell me about your Grandmother."

Bonnie drinks more wine and then begins to speak in English. Anton has never heard the language sound so musical, and he cannot take his eyes away from her lips. At last, she concludes: "My Grandmother was the only one who loved my brother and me. When I finally got away from home, my mother threw out everything I'd ever touched." She looks down again at the rabbit. "Where have you been all this time?"

Anton tries to recall where he got the book, but he is addled by adrenalin and alcohol and cannot. Nevertheless, he says, "I remember the house sale I got this from. I take you, show you. You will be pleased to know it came from a good home."

This is a lie worth telling to see Bonnie again. If he cannot remember the truth when he can think straight again, he will take her to see the prettiest house he knows.

Bonnie smiles, a line of tears cradled in each eye. "I leave Paris tomorrow."

Anton opens his mouth to protest, but no words come. With a heavy hand, he reaches for his brown paper and wraps the book carefully, trying to slow time and stop it forever at that moment. But the seconds tick by. When he has finished, the woman takes out her euros. Anton shakes his head. "I have merely been looking after it for you," he says.

Bonnie hugs the book to her chest, and Anton sees the child she had once been. She thanks him again and again, backing away, holding his gaze until she is forced to turn by the fast flowing crowd.

There is the familiar nibble of bereavement that comes with the loss of every book, but with each step she takes, his grief takes bigger bites. He is rooted to the spot, unable to summon the words to call her back, and he looks up at the sky in an instinctual plea for inspiration.

Once Bonnie is out of sight, it is already as if she had never existed. Anton looks down into his trunk, trying to find the space where the book had once been, but the fat serious volumes have already filled the gap—grateful that their silly little neighbor has left them more room to breathe. At the sight of them, he is filled with sorrow. He doubts any of them are capable of reproducing the kind of miracle that has just occurred. Lightning never strikes twice, so they say, and the books that remain are all sure to disappoint him in the end. Anton realizes he has been waiting all his working life for a customer like Bonnie.

"Where have you been all this time?" he says quietly to himself.

Just then, he feels something land upon his arm, a hand as light as a sparrow. There is Bonnie once more. His stomach flutters, like wind across the pages of a book.

"Perhaps we'll find each other again one day," she says.

Leaning in towards Anton, she plants a firm kiss on one side of his face and then the other, before she is swept away again by a surge of tourists, leaving behind wet spots on his cheeks that turn cold in the breeze coming off the Seine.

Author's Bio:

Lorna Partington Walsh is a British-born wordsmith who has been living in California for the past decade. She is a freelance editor and loves nothing more than helping authors to tell heart-centered stories and craft powerful prose. In her spare time, Lorna writes fiction, and she was nominated for the Pushcart Prize in 2017 for her short story "Becoming," which she is currently working into a novel.

Toby

By Debby Huvaere

I waived my right to an attorney. I wouldn't know who to call, and I don't really trust those state appointed lawyers. I've seen *How to Make a Murderer*.

The room is ill-lit. Some of the fluorescent bulbs are out, except for those directly above my head. The irony isn't lost on me. I don't belong in the light, but if light is antidote to darkness, I guess these cops need all they can get.

A year ago, I would have never imagined myself sitting in this chair, across a table facing a mirrored window. I know they're watching me, even though the room is empty. The detective left through a door behind me, to get me the soda I had asked for when he offered me a drink. I wanted to ask for coffee, but thought better of it. Isn't that what you hear in movies and read in books? That the police serve horrible coffee?

I stare at the manila folder, probably left to intimidate me, pale against the already sickening beige of the table top. It's thin though, and I guess that's a good thing. But something in there made them come for me and bring me to this station, and that understanding is why rivulets of sweat now run down my back.

I know I may *look* composed. I'm not worried about that. If anyone behind that window is making bets on how fast I'm going to crack, the odds are off. I'm used to working under pressure. Some people think accountancy is boring and uneventful, but they haven't known tax season like I do. My folded hands are steady and I give them a quick squeeze on the table where I've put them. I lean a bit forward, neither in defense nor defeat. I just wait for the detective and my drink, with feigned curiosity.

"9-1-1, what's your emergency?"

I don't expect that – to hear her voice. My eyes glance up in a quick reflex and meet those of the detective. The other one. They came back a pair, with my soda, which I don't touch. Susan Novak, she said her name was. Other than introducing herself, she hasn't spoken a word, just stares at me. I cast my eyes back down.

For a brief moment, I tell myself this isn't what I think it is, but then I hear the caller:

"Oh my god! He's not breathing! He... oh my god... 377 Forest Street! He's not breathing!"

My heart immediately speeds up and beats so hard, my ears start ringing. I know that voice. It's mine. The voices are coming from an iPhone the other detective – Giordano - has placed in the middle of the table. A video recorder will tape our conversation, he explained.

"Sir? I'm gonna need you to calm down, okay? Who's not breathing, sir?"
"My son... he's not... oh my god please HURRY!"

I don't remember sounding that whiny. Whenever I replay that call in my head, I always sound collected. Alarmed, sure, but calm and focused, wanting to save my son's life and certain I will.

"Your son isn't breathing? I have the address as 377 Forest Street, sir – is that correct?"
"He's not breathing! Oh my god... yes, yes! 377 Forrest, where are they!?"
"Sir, a team is on the way, okay? They'll be there shortly. Now I need you to listen to me and answer my questions, okay?"

I whimper an agreement on the tape and I wince. I want to yell at that guy to get his fucking shit together. But the guy is me, and it's too late, anyway.

"Sir, how old is your boy? Is he laying on the floor?"
"He's six... oh my god, he's only six, please!"
"I understand sir, we're gonna save your boy, okay? Has he fallen?"

There. There it is. A promise.

"Yes, he just... we were playing soccer... he collapsed... in the backyard... he's not breathing! We're in the back!"
"Okay, can you check for me sir, if his tongue is obstructing his throat?"
"I... I haven't... yes... no, no, his tongue is fine, oh my god, he's still not breathing. Toby! Toby!!"
"Sir, I need you to feel if he has a pulse, does Toby have a pulse? Can you check that for me? Just place your finger on his pulse or side of the neck, or feel his chest – is there a..."
"Yes! Yes – oh my god, I feel it."

My heart jumps as I hear joy seeping through tears. Hope. I recognize it. I relive it. I close my eyes and I think about my son…

He died. Toby. We didn't save him. The ambulance had come, and they tried, those guys. Pulled me away from his body. Someone told me I had to call my wife. But Teresa had passed away two years earlier. It was just me and my Toby, and my parents. I had called them on the way to the hospital.

My dad still maintained our garden, while mom took care of Toby, taking him to and from school. She had suggested we move to a smaller place in the city, but my therapist claimed staying was better for the both of us. I agreed. The idea of moving both tired and frightened me. To lose all of Theresa was too much. But now, I had lost the most important part of her.

A woman had come to the funeral. The woman whose voice I just listened to on the 911 call: Karen Smith. Just an ordinary name. She had introduced herself as the emergency dispatcher who had taken my call. Said she was so sorry for my loss. I couldn't say anything. The doctor had given me a tranquilizer and I was floating numbly through the entire service. She cried, Karen. My mother hugged her.

*

"Can you tell us what day this is, Mister Brodsky?" the detective asks — the guy, Giordano. I swallow. The can of Sprite soda stands unopened before me. Condensation is forming a dark circle on the table. I don't think now is a good time to open it. Such a nonchalant gesture right before stating what they already must know.

"That's the day my son died," I say, "five months ago." My voice sounds strange, as if it's too big for my head, as if it is pressing to escape my ears, too.

"Do you know who you spoke to that day? Who the emergency dispatcher was?"

I realize I'm still staring at the soda can. I divert my eyes to my folded hands.

"She came to the funeral," I whisper. It's the truth. Neither of them speak for a while. It's probably only seconds, but it feels like minutes. I feel I should add something, but I know it's a tactic. They want me to talk, the more the better. I urge myself not to fidget, keep my eyes focused on an upright hair on my knuckle. Maybe I should have gotten a lawyer.

The female detective, Novak, puts her hand on the manila folder, pulls it closer. It scratches over the surface. I still don't look up.

"Do you know her name, Mr. Brodsky?" Giordano is the one breaking the silence. A slight victory.

"Karen. Karen Smith," I say.

*

I had looked her up, the night of the funeral, after everyone had gone. I assured my mother I'd be fine and she reluctantly followed my dad out the front door. The house was quiet, a different kind of quiet than what I was used to. Not the peaceful stillness I sometimes embraced when I had put Toby to bed and I could grab a beer and watch some TV. It was as if the entire house had stopped breathing, when he did. It was both unbearably hollow and impossible to puncture it with any noise. I couldn't even stand the thought of music.

First, I just Googled her, but there were a lot of Karen Smiths. I had better luck on Facebook. She popped up on top of the list, probably because we had about thirty friends in common. My mother had told me the woman's boy was in Toby's class. She had shared an article about Toby, one that appeared in the local Gazette,

I hadn't known about. My mom must have kept the papers away from me:

Local Boy Dies of Heart Failure.

It had been a condition he had had. Nobody had ever detected it, because six-year-old hearts aren't supposed to fail. It was a tragedy, they said. Nothing to be done.

My finger had hovered over the "friend" button. Part of me wanted to connect with this woman with whom I shared such a traumatic experience. She and I were oddly connected through the tragedy. But then, a voice roared in my head and yelled, *she promised!* I lifted my finger. She had failed to keep her promise. She was *not* my friend.

*

"Mister Brodsky… We're dealing with a very disturbing disappearance," Giordano continues, "and we have reason to believe you have something to do with that."

I raise my brows and look him in the eye. "I'm not sure I understand."

Giordano turns his head to his colleague and nods subtly. Detective Novak picks up the manila folder off the table and opens it. I can't see its contents as she shifts through some papers. When she finds what she's looking for, she plucks it from the folder. Before she places it in front of me, I already know what it is.

"We found this in a backpack, belonging to Cain Smith," she says. "Cain is the six-year-old son of Miss Karen Smith – the emergency dispatcher you spoke to the afternoon your son passed away."

The note is a folded yellow piece of paper that reads:

You're not going to be able to save him either.

I look at her with confusion. Confusion is appropriate in this moment. Confusion is what I feel.

"Mister Brodsky, Cain has been missing for almost a week now. Perhaps you can help us find him?"

*

The night of the funeral, I had eventually fallen asleep on the couch, tired of clicking through the woman's Facebook feed. She had a husband and three children. Pictures of a happy family, with captions explaining why.

I recognized her from the photos two months later when she was walking towards a Target as I was walking out. I had gone and bought bins to put Toby's stuff in because everyone had kept insisting I move on. She didn't recognize me, walked right by, laughing. Laughing!

I looked at her profile again that night. Posts had been added, each of them depicting a life so joyous, mine paled in comparison, even vanished. This woman had promised to save my son, wept at his funeral and then simply moved on, because she could. My son's death was just a blip to her existence, while it made mine worthless. How was that fair?

*

Her boy had been there, the afternoon I went to the school to pick up Toby's things that had been left behind: a hat, some artwork, the toy police car he'd gotten for his birthday. It all fit in a shoebox his teacher handed me in a near deserted hallway. Meanwhile, behind the classroom door, I could make out a dozen or so kids growing louder.

"My after school arts program," she explained, "I better get back in. They have clay."

I asked her where I could find the restroom. She pointed and I accepted the look of pity she gave me and made my way down the corridor. I noticed kids' name tags above hooks along the wall. Toby's hook was empty. Further up the line, I saw a *Cain Smith,* where a blue jacket hung under a yellow backpack. The color was so vivid and vibrant, as if to mock me; the backpack of a kid very much alive.

In the restroom, I splashed cold water on my face. Stared at my reflection in the mirror above the sink. I opened the cross-body bag I always had on me, took out a small pad of paper and wrote the note. I was just going to leave a note. A reminder to Karen Smith that life was precious, that it could be taken away.

The boy stood outside the classroom when I returned to leave the note. I froze in my track, as if I'd been caught. I realized who he was.

"Time out," he shrugged, nonchalantly.

"I see," I said. The note folded in my hand, his yellow backpack close, but unapproachable. I could have walked away. But how unsatisfied would that have left me? I crouched down instead. "Wanna go for ice cream?" I asked.

The boy's eyes first grew, then immediately narrowed in realization that I was the stranger he wasn't supposed to talk to.

"It's okay," I smiled. "I'm Toby's dad."

He grew sad. "Toby is my friend." He mumbled.

"I see. Must have been a good friend?"

"The best!" The boy lifted his chin.

"I would love to hear more about your friendship," I spoke with a lump in my throat. "So why don't you tell me all about it over a sundae, huh?" I rose back up to my feet and felt myself lift a backpack from the hook and reach my hand out to the boy. He didn't hesitate anymore. Walking out of that school, yellow backpack in my one hand and a warm small hand in the other, I recalled all I had lost.

*

"Mister Brodsky?"

It's detective Novak who wakes me from my reverie. I was just going to put a note in a backpack, just a threat to make that woman understand how everything is fragile. I feel like I should explain. Words are bubbling up inside me. I'm eager to form sentences that reason, plead and justify.

"I'll show you where the body is," I tell them.

Author's Bio:

Debby Huvaere is a writer and award-winning screenwriter. Her work appears in the Montclair Write Group Anthology, and is upcoming at Raining On Rooftops Review.

Originally from Belgium, she currently lives in Montclair, New Jersey.

Running Man

By Desiree Kannel

Robin knew what she was doing was silly, but she did it anyway. She turned her car into the Jack 'n the Box parking lot. And there was, the perfect spot just waiting for her. Facing the street, Robin pulled her car to a stop, turned off the ignition but left the key in. The lot was about a block from the bus stop, making it a perfect place to look for him, the *running man* — the man she had seen yesterday, but had ignored. The man she couldn't stop thinking about.

Yesterday

She had been waiting at a red light, when a man dashed by her car window. It didn't take her long to figure out he was running after a bus, the one that had just turned the corner at the opposite end of the intersection. From her vantage point, Robin could tell he wouldn't make it. He was running after something he'd never catch. She watched him maneuver through the intersection and was impressed at how he stayed focused on his goal, ignored the drivers that braked, honked, and flipped him off. She glanced up and saw the short line of passengers making their way onto the bus. After the last one disappeared inside, the engine revved, and a cloud of black exhaust greeted the running man just as he made it to the curb a short distance away from the bus. Yet, he kept running. He yanked off his jacket and frantically waved it above his head. Robin imagined he was yelling, "Stop!" or "Wait!" but she knew he would be wasting his breath. They never wait. Bus drivers have schedules to keep.

The whole scene mesmerized her and it took the blast of a few car horns to shake off the trance. Autos in the next lane pulled forward through the intersection and glanced in her direction. Robin took a deep breath, then drove forward.

When she reached the other side of the intersection, her foot lifted off the gas pedal and she let her car coast towards the bus stop. The running man was there, sitting on the blue bench, his jacket slung over his left shoulder. She imagined herself coming to a quick stop right in front of him. "Get in!" She'd shout through the open window. "I'll take you to the next stop." She would smile too, so he'd know she was serious.

She didn't stop and twenty minutes later, she pulled into the driveway of the home she shared with Scott, her husband. She sat in the driveway listening to the tick-tick-tick of the cooling car, regretting a conversation she never had:

"Thanks!" The running man said, sliding into the front seat.

"No problem!"

"Not too many kind people anymore; lucky for me you came by!"

"Glad to help!"

She wasn't sure why they would be shouting at each other. Probably because the windows would still be down, and due to heavy traffic that time of day, it'd be a noisy drive.

Glad to help.

Robin tilted her head back on the head rest and closed her eyes. "I should have helped him," she whispered. A few minutes passed before she could bring herself to leave the car and her running man fantasy. She wouldn't need to use her imagination to know what was happening inside her home. Her husband, Scott, would be occupying the same space she had left him in that morning—he'd be sitting at his computer, researching grad programs.

"Searching for the right school is like a job itself," he had told her. "Especially one that's funded." He wrapped up his plea with the *now is the perfect time argument*, but looked past her when he added, "Since . . . you know."

Robin picked bits of arugula from her pizza and watched her husband finish off his third slice. In exchange for taking a leave of absence to focus on his "grad" search, Scott had agreed to take over dinner preparations. Robin had failed to make sure he knew the difference between preparing and ordering, so they ended up eating delivery at least twice a week. She put that on the list of issues to discuss with him, along with her continued hatred of arugula. She stopped eating it when she was pregnant, and three failed pregnancies later, the bitter taste still remains.

"There was this poor man running after a bus today." She started, as she removed the limp green leaves to the side of her plate. "But he missed it. I should have helped him."

Scott shook his head. "Not your problem. If he missed that one, he'll catch the next one."

"But what if he was on his way to something important? Like a job interview? Or a doctor's appointment?"

Scott dropped a rind of crust on his plate. "If it was so important, he should have lined-up more reliable transportation. Like Uber."

"Buses *are* reliable. And it's all some people have. Did you know that world-wide, owning a car puts you in the top ten percent of wealthy people?"

"Where did you hear that?"

She couldn't remember, maybe from a poli-sci professor she had freshman year.

"Never mind." Her appetite suddenly gone, she got up to clear the table. Even though her running man fantasy continued, she decided not to try and discuss it with Scott. She'd keep it all to herself, and then later, after she fixed everything—she'd find that man, apologize, and give him a ride to where ever he needed to go — then she would tell Scott. Talking about it to him now would be a waste of time. He, like everyone else, had adopted the practice of ignoring her. Especially when she got *emotional.* The therapist told her it was because people felt inadequate and unsure of what to say. She didn't want them to say anything, but acting like it hadn't happened is what hurt the most.

*

Back at the parking lot: seven minutes passed and every kind of car and pedestrian went by the Jack 'n the Box, but not her running man. *I saw you running after the bus yesterday and just wanted to say sorry for not stopping to give you a lift.* That's what she'd say to him. She'd get out of her car, casual like she was going to get something to eat. She hadn't figure out how she'd get their eyes to meet. Maybe she'd act surprised and say, *Hey! Didn't I see you running after a bus yesterday?* She played the scene out in her head, but couldn't get past her apology line. She was an hour late getting home, and then she lied to her husband.

"I hope they pay you overtime," he said. "Dinner's ready. Pasta."

The next day, Robin left work 30 minutes earlier. "Doctor's appointment," she told her coworkers, knowing it was a safe lie. In the elevator, on the way to the parking garage, a pinch of guilt surprised her. Screw them, she thought and exited the elevator.

She and Scott had used the saying, "third times the charm," a lot during that first and fragile trimester. It went from cute saying, to prayer, and then a plea.

After sitting in the Jack n' the Box parking lot for about half an hour, the futility of what she was attempting to do, crept in. A sarcastic laugh burst from her lips, when she thought of what her therapist would say. How obvious can you get? Robin chided herself as she got out of the car. The idea of eating had never occurred to her, but she was looking for a way to pass the time, while she waited for her running man. Leftover arugula covered pizza, bland pasta, and a husband she was trying not to hate, were the only things waiting for her back home.

Fast food had dropped out of Robin's life after she had met Scott during her first year of college. The campus was in full protest mode with the SPCA as the cause of the month. The quad was packed with students protesting everything from horse racing to factory farming. It's where she met Scott. He was dressed as a jersey cow, wearing a sign that read: DON'T EAT ME. He was handing out apples. "Thanks," she said taking a Granny Smith from his outstretched hoof-hand. Dating Scott was easy. She admired his passion; a quality her family felt overrated and unnecessary. Scott listened to stations like NPR and yelled at the radio, whenever someone with an opposing opinion came on. He took her to his meetings—small groups of fellow students pumped up on activist energy and hummus. Coming from a family whose passion only flared when the cable went out, it was easy to slip into Scott's life; his passion became her own and she found herself rallying for actions, anxious over problems she hadn't even known existed. *The bees are dying!*

Marrying him had been easy too. She looked back now and saw how she had been operating under some sort of meet-a-guy-and-get-married auto-pilot mode. No thought. All do. And then it was done. And then they both had jobs, and then the only thing left was to have children. That's when she started to pay attention.

They had had real conversations about how adding a baby into their lives, would change things. Their plans, although lacking in originality, seemed doable and gave them something to look forward too. But what happened, once, then twice, and then a third time was something neither had planned for. After the last miscarriage, Scott reasoned that he "might as well" get his PhD, which left Robin with only one option: go back to work. Close friends and her mother told her "staying busy" with work would be the best thing, and it was. Just not for her.

She entered the brightly colored fast food venue. A middle-aged woman stood behind the counter, her hands poised over the screen, ready to tap in the next customer's request. She looked like she could work the counter in her sleep.

"Can I help you?"

Robin realized how hungry she was when she scanned the menu. "I'll have a Jumbo Jack. Make that the combo."

"For here or to go?"

"Here."

Tray in hand, Robin walked to the back and slid into a booth next to the window. She picked up the burger. It was warm, soft, and heavier than she remembered. She peeled off the wrapper, thinking she would only eat half of it, if that much. Just holding it felt like cheating, or liberating. She couldn't decide. She closed her eyes and took a bite. Meat, grease and memories flooded her senses.

The food tasted better than she imagined it would, or maybe she was just hungry. Either way, the only things left on her tray were grease stained wrappers and depleted catsup packages. She had devoured the entire meal without even stopping to think. She surveyed the remnants, accepted the fact that a bout of queasiness would soon follow, and decided it didn't matter. A sigh slipped from her lips, coming out louder than she had intended. The customer in the booth opposite her, chuckled. "Must have been good. I didn't know fast food could be that satisfying."

Robin felt her cheeks warm, not sure if it was from embarrassment or a reaction to the meal. She tilted her chin up to see who had been observing, and saw her running man looking right back at her.

Author's Bio:

Desiree is a writer and teacher from Long Beach, California. She is the owner of Rose Writers Workshops and leads creative writing workshops for adults and teens. Her work has appeared online and Running for a Bus is her first major publication. A Long Beach native, Desiree is helping to develop the Long Beach Literary Arts Center; a nonprofit with the goal of making her hometown a literary powerhouse! Follow Desiree @RWwrites

The Lucky Ones

By Molly Byrne

"Come out fuck face," Trinity yells. She's looking for me. I am under the stairs, trying to figure out why I don't feel like going Upstate this year. It's summer, and who wouldn't be looking forward to a tiny cabin packed with every foster kid we've ever had? Not that I ever look forward to going anywhere. I hope Trinity doesn't come down here, because she already found out about the roof and the closet. Pretty soon nowhere will be safe.

"Lou?" She calls. She's closer now.

Last year, on my fifteenth birthday, Trinity started calling me Lou Gehrig and since my dad was home then, it caught on. He apparently forgot that he had named me after Louis Armstrong, because art was the most important thing. It seems like he forgets a lot of stuff he told me. Like we didn't have a whole life together.

I wait for her to pass by the stairs. Her footsteps creak on the floorboards, even though Trinity always walks on the balls of her feet as if she's tiptoeing. I wish she would go away. I wish I didn't wish that.

Trinity pauses. She's breathing quietly through her nose. That is how she learned to breathe when she was hiding from her dad. *Not everyone is lucky enough to have a family like ours,* Mom would say. Trinity's therapy session is right before mine and sometimes I can hear them talking, if Dr. Hugo leaves the door ajar. I breathe through my nose too. I imagine for a moment that I'm hiding from something dangerous, instead of Trinity. I imagine I have a reason to feel the fear rise in my throat.

She opens the door, and I realize that maybe I've gasped out loud. She sees me lying there and she cocks her head to one side, as if deciding. Then she steps inside and lies down, so she's stretched out next to me. It's like you're hiking alone and you suddenly see a deer and for a second, it stands still and trusts, but you can't move because as soon as you do it's going to run. I hold still under the stairs, feeling Trinity next to me with the hairs of my arms. I don't move at all. After only a few moments she says, "You're a goddamn freak," and gets to her feet. As she leaves, she tells me, "She needs you to pack the car." I nod so she knows I heard her. She doesn't close the door on her way out.

Upstairs, I dodge the twins as they ricochet off a wall and leave splatters behind of whatever grime they have recently rolled in. The house is golden with summer afternoon sunshine, with yellow walls and wood floors. I go into the bathroom, where the small window only lets in a single shady shaft of blue daylight. I sit on the toilet seat and put my head in my hands, but only for a minute before I hear the telltale floorboards creak.

"I'm in here!" I yell, but it's Mitch. Mitch is the baby; he doesn't know anything about privacy, and his therapist says he probably never will. He peeks around the door, his too-wide eyes blinking at me, smiling without teeth.

"Wou!" he exclaims, sidling into the room. He immediately starts picking up toothbrushes and putting them back down, making me nervous.

"Louis!" I hear from a distance, and even if I didn't recognize the particular shrill cadence of her voice, I would know that it's Mom because nobody else calls me Louis anymore.

It's seconds before she's in the doorway, glowing as she always does when we are about to go on a trip. "Oh Mitch," she coos. She picks him up and smells his diaper. I hold still, because sometimes I can ride under her radar if she gets distracted enough. It doesn't work this time. She tosses her words over her shoulder, as she starts changing the diaper. "Can you help me?" she asks. I wonder if she knows how many times she has said that to me, with the exact same lock of hair flopping over her forehead, the same sheen of sweat on the bridge of her nose, and the same half-wild look in her eyes. It's not a question, not when Mom asks. It's an accusation. Her eyes drill into me, *for once?*

I'd love to be brave and point out every other time I've packed the car or changed a diaper or cleaned the house because someone else was having an emergency. I wish I could start a fight right here, right now, by having my own meltdown. But in the end, even though admitting my cowardice and how it hurts deeply, I get up. I don't have a choice.

"We are almost ready to go, can you just pack the car?" she speaks without looking at me, "I don't know how you're going to do it this time, it's a lot of stuff!"

I walk through the house where walls are smeared at kid-level. Mom likes to say our house looks "lived in". When I go through the front door, the broken screen door slams shut behind me. The torn screen needs fixing.

We are the kind of misfit family that the kids at school don't invite on their ski weekends. It doesn't help when Saturdays are spent waiting your turn for therapy, even if you're only there because Mom doesn't want anyone to get special treatment. If you walk down our street, you see suburban houses with their ornamental columns and manicured lawns and then you come to our house, which looks like a prison yard, provided all the inmates are children. Our lawn is weed and gravel, with a number of rusty trucks and faded plastic slides gathered out front.

The only nice bit is the vegetable garden, which is Trinity's. Mom says it's helping her find peace. I can understand that. I look for peace there too sometimes, even if I never find it. I guess it's different when the tomatoes are yours and yours alone. We used to have a grassy yard and a swing set. When I was really little, Mom used to take me outside and push me as high as she could. I would ask for higher and higher and when it got too high, she would suddenly stop the swing and hug me so tightly, I thought I might explode and we'd both laugh. You're not supposed to touch kids who have experienced trauma, and now, because of the "no special treatment" rule, that means me too, even though I'm not like the others.

In the driveway, the minivan is already open, its trunk gaping at me, every door ajar. There are piles of bags so haphazard, they appear to have been flung out the second story window. I survey them all for a moment. The sun makes the back of my neck itch. There's an art to packing. You see all the things laid out and then have to find the ways they can fold into a space. Normally, I like the challenge. It's different this time because the last thing I want to do is go on this trip. Not that it matters. Even Dad has to be there, so there is no way *I'm* getting out of it.

I should be excited to see him. Dad's been away for ages, and when we talk on the phone the connection is crackly because he's somewhere in the African bush saving lives. I know I should be excited. But then again, I can't remember the last time I was excited about anything. Mom can't either, and she's always telling me "life is good Louis" as though maybe, if she says it enough, I'll realize I've been happy this whole time.

When I finish packing, I wait. I have to pee, but I don't want to go back inside, so I wander over to the vegetable garden and unzip. Our neighbor Burton, who watches our house all the time so he can keep an eye on how much his property value decreases day by day, opens his window when I'm halfway through sprinkling the tomato plants.

"That's public indecency," he yells. I think I've committed enough crimes in our yard that if Burton were ever to be a cop, he'd have more arrests than anyone on my account. I flip him off and he closes the window, but I know he's still watching. He's *pervy* like that. I was about nine when I learned about pedophiles in school. I told Mom Burton looked at me funny, but she only laughed, because that was the year we had two kids in our home who had had more than just funny looks from men with mustaches.

"There's always a fire with you, isn't there?" she said.

I wander back to the car, and put my hands on either side of my head, which throbs. I might have a brain tumor. A belching squelching cancerous mass strangling whatever part of my brain is responsible for smiling. Sometimes I wish I had a tumor. Although even a brain tumor couldn't convince Mom to let me stay home. I sit down on the pavement behind the minivan, the hot metal of the bumper digging into my back. It is almost quiet out here; just the sound of a distant mower. I hear the front door slam.

Mom comes around the side of the van with a box. I've just finished packing, and we both know it, but she just puts one hip out and stares at me. She lets the box hit the ground, daring me to say something about it. I look at the familiar curve of her lip, wondering how a person can put so much expectation into a single facial expression.

"It won't fit." I tell her.

"You can do it." There she goes again, believing in me.

"I can't."

She rolls her eyes. She's got her running shoes on, which she never runs in. She stares at me appraisingly for a second and then crouches beside me. Rummaging in her pocket, she pulls out a bag of fruit gummies. I squint at her. She pops a strawberry in her mouth, and holds the bag, but I don't take one.

"He can't wait to see you." She says. She's looking at me real closely.

"I know." I say. Of course he can't.

Mom eats a peach gummy. "You're one of the lucky ones." She says, another familiar line.

I sigh. I can't help it. She notices.

"You are." She repeats, and then, true to script, her voice softens: "Kylie, Mitch, Trinity." She says each of their names with a heavy emphasis, implying their unluckiness. Every time a new kid comes to live with us, she gives me the same speech. *You're lucky to have an uneventful childhood. You're lucky you don't need special attention.*

I can't look at her. I just nod. She gets up and claps her hands together, as though everything has been decided. I'm looking down so I don't see it coming, but as she turns to go back in the house she touches my hair, so quickly I don't have time to react. Then she snatches her hand back, afraid she might get stung. She heads back into the house.

"We're just about ready!" She says cheerily. It's quiet again for only about five seconds before the door slams open and the twins barrel out toward the street. I reflexively intercept them, shepherding them into the car. I buckle their seatbelts over their fat tummies, trying to harness them as fast as I can. Trinity comes outside, carrying Mitch.

"Shotgun." She hollers, and I shoot her a grateful glance because I don't think I'd survive the drive with Mom's meaningful gaze at me, while forgetting to watch the road. Trinity hands me Mitch and

I get the belt all sorted out. He undoes it. I buckle it. He unbuckles it. We go back and forth until Mom hops in the front seat, all noise and energy, holding more bags and snacks.

"Let's go! Who's excited?" Mom chirps. The twins yell, Trinity makes a small, self-conscious whoop, and Mitch gurgles. I buckle him while he's distracted. Then I get in the way back, the final box on the seat next to me. I scrunch down so Mom won't see I have my earbuds in. She rolls all the windows down and starts singing. I close my eyes.

It wasn't always this way. The first year we made this trip, it was just me and Mom, and Mom let me sit up front because she didn't want to be alone, which isn't the kind of good parenting she's famous for. I was seven, and propped up on about six pillows, but the seatbelt still dug into my cheek. Mom wasn't singing then, she was taking long shaky breaths, nodding occasionally to some inner monologue I couldn't hear, and wiping her palms on her pant legs. I don't think she knows I remember that.

We stop at a rest- stop halfway. Mom takes Mitch inside. Trinity and I gingerly check on the twins, but they're asleep, lulled to passivity by the movement of the van. Trinity rummages in a bag and pulls out a package of Twinkies. I eye her down, but she pretends she can't see me. She slowly peels back the wrapper, trying to keep it from crinkling. She takes a bite and rolls her eyes in ecstasy, takes a long time chewing, her mouth half open so I can see the gruesome mastication of cream and cake. I laugh, silently.

"*What's up*?" She mouths at me. She looks out the window behind my head, avoiding eye contact while she talks. It's an old tic she still can't shake. I shrug. She holds out a fist with a thumb; first pointing it up, then letting it wobble to the side. For a second her eyes catch mine, meaningful, and she lets her thumb start pointing down. She looks at me, asking a question with her eyes and her hand. I hold out my own thumb and wiggle it about halfway in response.

"*Meh*?" she asks, barely a murmur. A sleeping twin snorts a little and we freeze for a second.

"*Meh*," I reply.

She smiles, which lights up her whole face, and tosses me a Twinkie. Mom opens the door to deposit Mitch. *Meh* is our base state, Trinity and me. We've been *meh* after therapy and before it, *meh* on our birthdays and *meh* at funerals. It's the one thing we can agree on. I hide my Twinkie, so I won't have to share with Mitch.

*

It's late afternoon when we arrive, but we've managed to catch the sunset, which is vivid over the bay. It's colder up here, and invisible gnats buzz in and out of my ears. I release the kids from their shackles and I let them take off, because here they have some room to run. Mom grabs bags from the backseat. She's smiling in that giddy, flustered way she gets when she's about to see *him.*

I fumble with duffels in the backseat as the front door of the house opens. I hear him exclaim, in his booming voice, "My disciples!" which he thinks is funny, but isn't. I picture the way he is holding his arms out, and how he'll be scanning us over, looking for something.

"Madalena!" He yells, and Mom, the gazelle, practically leaps towards him, her head high and eyes shining. I keep my head down. "Lou!" He yells, but I don't look. I don't move toward him. I can hear the weariness behind his bluster. "My boy!" he adds, and the note of uncertainty in his voice makes me turn around. He's smiling at me, sheepishly. He's grown a beard since last I'd last seen him, and he has crinkles in his forehead that betray him as a man who frowns more than he laughs, though he pretends otherwise. He stands there, one arm around Mom, one arm stretched out to the side, where I should go. I don't move. I should go stand next to him, but I can't. Our eyes lock. Mom always says how we have the same eyes.

I see right through him, and I know that he has been smiling to Mom's face, nodding, exclaiming and yelling like he is supposed to, for years. Pretending to be in love with it all. Pretending that he doesn't lie awake wondering what it all means. I stare him down. It's only a matter of time before the charade ends. Before she realizes that whatever cynicism I have is genetic. I got it from him. Mom laughs off my reticence.

"These teenagers, they'll be the death of us," she says, shaking her head at me, but she is practically bouncing with happiness, so the insult doesn't stick. The twins collide with him now, and he sweeps them up in his arms. He used to do that to me too, when I was little. When I still believed he was happiest at home with us.

"Trinity," he says, more subdued because with Trinity you have to be. Trinity is laden with duffels as well, and she nods at him, looking past him to the door.

"Kenneth," she replies, which is the most she's ever said to him. Mom beams so brightly she might explode, because that is the sort of thing she likes to call a breakthrough. She lives for these moments.

Trinity and I are standing in front of the door now. I am sweating, she's folded her arms across her chest, and finally Mom gives a little laugh and pushes open the door. Trinity and I follow, unburdening ourselves in the doorway. Mom grabs Trinity by the shoulders, which Trinity endures without wincing (last month's breakthrough).

"C'mon Trin, let's set up the girl's room!" Mom says as she bounds up the narrow pine stairs. The ceiling is oppressive in the cabin, but the light is dim, cool, and fading. He sidles in behind the kitchen island. We stand across from one another for a moment, quiet now that no one else is around.

"You in school?" he asks, a weird question for a father to ask, but Dad never claimed to be normal.

"School's good. How's Africa?" I ask. I don't want to be rude.

"Really well, we have almost ninety percent inoculated..." He trails off, and I can't tell if it's because he's realized that I'm not interested or that he's not. "It's good to be back with you guys," he finishes, lamely.

I hear the twins yelling and I look out the window, where the bay is sparkling and the sky is blood red and the lawn is un-mowed and waving. He clears his throat.

"They need me over there," he starts to say. I keep to myself. "Buddy, I'm always here for you. If you need me" he says. Which means Mom has been talking to him about me.

"Yep," I blurt, hoping he'll stop and save us both the awkwardness. He gets the hint. He looks like he wants to do something else, but we've never really gone in for affection.

Mom and Trinity come down the stairs.

"Well let's start dinner!" Mom says, laughing. As they begin the fumbling of pots and pans, I sneak back out the door. I hear the door slam a second time and I turn to see Trinity a step behind me, her braids alive in the wind off the bay.

"Where are you going?" she accuses as she reaches me, her head cocked, her arms crossed.

I shrug, digging a toe in the dirt, uprooting a waving tuft of grass.

"Seriously?" she says, putting a hand on her hips.

"Do you remember what Mom used to be like?" I ask. It's abrupt, but Trinity and I have a different sort of language. The setting sun creates a rosy blush on her face.

"Depressed?" she quips.

"Just not...like this."

"She's happy now."

"But she used to be..." I trail off. I don't even know what I mean.

"She used to be inches away from a breakdown. At least she and

Kenneth have figured it out." Trinity says matter-of-factly. She doesn't like subtext. She's still peering at me, wondering what I am really asking.

"Figured it out? As in figured out they can't stand being on the same continent?"

Trinity shrugs, "It works for them."

"Doesn't work for me," I say. I know I sound whiny. I wait for her to roll her eyes and say something snarky back, but she doesn't say anything.

We both look out over the bay, because the sunset is really glaring off the water now, and it's hard to keep your eyes off it. We stand there and our ears are filled with the sounds of the approaching night; crickets and frogs and owls. I feel a chill, even though it's not cold yet, and I shiver. Trinity shifts. Maybe it's because of the sunset, or because of the trip, or maybe it's just because Trinity knows what it's like to need someone, but all of a sudden she puts an arm around me, and puts her head on my shoulder. I am so surprised I hold still. I don't hug her back like I should. Maybe I've forgotten how.

She doesn't say all the things I should know; that our family is doing so much better, we have a lot of love to give, that the grass always seems greener, even when it's not. She doesn't say any of that because she knows I know.

She just stays there and sways slightly and hugs me until my shoulder starts to soften. Then, as abruptly as it began, she lets go. She gives me a godfather pat on the cheek, a "whatcha-gonna-do" smile, and turns to go back inside. She doesn't tell me to follow. I watch her skip up the steps, and for a moment I almost wish I was skipping with her.

The sun has slipped almost all the way gone and the dusk is turning gray, a sort of colorless fog you could disappear into. It's quiet out here, except for the cicadas. I walk down by the rocky coast, through a stand of bony pines. Down by the shore, where the water is receding and the mud stinks of seaweed and old fish, I duck under the dock. It's an old hiding place no one has found yet. It's damp and smelly, and it only appears when the tide is out. I lay down. The rock is cold through my shirt.

A Friend's Text

By Jenn Powers

What she really has is like the last good day of summer when she doesn't know it's the last good day of summer. There's an unknown cutoff line. He keeps her wrapped up like a pretty gift with nothing in it. His stare fluctuates between adoration and disdain. It's like a drafty attic in November. He's older, he's always older, and he always has lots of money. He's a tiny-eyed, coppery golfer. He wears those pin-striped suits, those four months' worth of rent suits, and a flimsy crimson tie whipping in the wind like a dragon's tongue. He never wears his wedding ring, which she loves, until she spots the matching gold bands in a family portrait on social media. She tells herself not to look—but she always does.

Thing is, he gets her. He supports her acting career in ways no one else does. He cheers her on. He's a risk-taker too. Look how far he's come. Look at his success. And he tells her to keep going, keep chasing, keep working, how mediocre minds never understand artistic pursuits. His support cancels out the hurt when she's alone, while he's on dates with his wife. And then, there's the way he rests his head on her lap in the back of the limo, the way he convinces her he can't live without her.

She grew up to believe: you don't date millionaires. They exist in some alternate universe far away from working class suburbia. It's like finding a unicorn. The closest she'd ever get was inside her childhood imagination. The idyllic world of Ken and Barbie, equipped with matching Corvettes. Flamingo pink mansion. Essentially, forget it kid. Stick to what you know. Kool-Aid, dirt, and sunshine. Hand-me-downs, toys from the flea market, milk toast. Live paycheck to paycheck. It's honorable. It's respectable to struggle.

But twenty years later, the unicorn shows up.

He finds her on social media. He asks her out to lunch. He orders a bottle of private label wine. He wears an Italian silk tie the color of tropical waters. She's accustomed to Carhartt and Coors, bonfires and 24-hour diners, not this pretty man dipped in gold. He tells her he's married, but things aren't going so well. She glimpses his starched white collar, glitzy wristwatch. He stands out like an exotic plant against the snowy hills and bare trees. He says he hopes to see her again soon. He hops into his silver Aston Martin. She imagines it smells like his cologne and new leather, not like the jalopies she rode in as a kid. Those pea green Olds classmates would make fun of the rust above the wheels and lap seatbelts so hot, they burned her thighs.

She debates with her conscience. It's wrong, wrong, *wrong*. Somehow, he reaches inside and takes something without asking. She wants a peek inside that fantasyland. She wants to enter, like when Alice finds the tiny door to the garden. They go to Gramercy Park Hotel every other week: sapphire blue armchairs, art by Warhol and Damien Hirst, crystal glasses of Macallan scotch whiskey. Velvet drapes enclose them into a secret world where he peppers her with: "Meeting you is a catalyst," "I've never reacted like this to anyone," and "You're so easy to talk to." She senses the irreversible change scribbling all over her once simplistic life. "You've been missing from my life. Quit your job. Travel with me." She floats between seaside mansions and skyscraper hotels. West Palm Beach. Los Angeles.

Newport. Boston. Scottsdale. Mostly, New York City. Poached eggs under silver domes. Spa bathrobes. Turndown service.

Friends push back. They ask why they can't meet him, what's the big secret, what's she hiding, and so she becomes scarce. He keeps telling her to be patient, and after three years, she can no longer fight the fact that it's never progressed. He becomes distant. Like a hunk of ice stuck in her chest. She shakes a little. She hasn't met anyone on his side and he hasn't met anyone on hers. She wants more. She wants to show him where she bought five-cent fireballs as a kid, where she took swimming lessons. She wants him at her birthday party and college graduation and Thanksgiving dinner. She wants to force-feed him her life: *Look! This is me. This is my life.*

He stays out late and later. She awakens alone in a dim, gigantic, cold hotel room, around midnight—to the click of the lock. He slides into the room. His jacket is beaded with sleet. He has an icy, distant stare, like *oh, you're still here*, and she feels the cold run through her. Earlier that day, she had found out about a third woman, a fourth woman, and he is, in fact, still banging his wife. She had scoured his laptop and found the emails, while he was at a meeting downtown.

The last time. They check out of Gramercy Park Hotel. She watches him easily leave without looking back to where she stands. She stops at an underground coffee shop for a blueberry scone and jasmine green tea. She fingers the stack of hundreds in her wallet. It's bitter cold outside. She opens her suitcase to retrieve the gloves, the ones with the white fur trim, the ones he bought for her on a whim at Bergdorf's. She sniffs them: the hotel room: magnolia soap, room service coffee, starched bedsheets. Something sinks inside—but she knows it's good. Pain can be right.

He owns companies. She passes his building, a gold glass building that reflects the cityscape around her. She can't look at herself. She's better than this. She soldiers onward, alone, to the bus station. The inevitable breakup is heavy in her back pocket. She looks up at the sky for a sign. Instead, her phone beeps. She hurries to check it. It's a text from a girlfriend she's known since childhood: ARE YOU OKAY?

She cracks and takes a seat on a bench. *Am I okay?* It's been so long since someone has asked that—especially him. She doesn't know how to respond. She and her friend made their First Holy Communion together at Saint Mary's Church in their hometown. She wore a second-hand dress made of cotton with eyelets bordering the neckline. Her mother made her a crown of daisies from the backyard. She remembers cartwheels and green grass, living room forts and whole wheat pancakes; the ugly pea green jalopy the kids made fun of; the hand-me-downs, crocheted blankets, cats at the foot of the bed. She longs for home, for something real, for the contentment that has absolutely nothing to do with being rich.

Author's Bio:

Jenn Powers is a writer and visual artist from New England. She is currently at work on two psychological thrillers, one with elements of sci-fi. She has work published or forthcoming in CutBank, Blue Mesa Review, Gris-Gris, Spillway, The Pinch, Jabberwock Review, Thin Air, and Hayden's Ferry Review, among others, and she has been nominated for a Pushcart Prize. Please visit www.jennpowers.com for more information.

Desert Rats

By Gary Kidney

The school bus to Dos Padres Junior High stopped at the trailer park's corner in the middle of the Arizona desert. I thought it funny because I didn't have a father, let alone two. I know how it works. A man had to have made me. But he wasn't more than a sperm donor, abandoning me when I was four — eight and a half years ago.

I was afraid of seventh grade — new teachers, schedule, cafeteria food, and bigger boys to poke fun at me. I dreaded them most. At the bus stop, there was group of rowdy boys, cussing, telling dirty jokes, teasing girls, and tossing a football. They called their gang Desert Rats. I prayed they wouldn't notice me.

"Pee, will you keep me invisible?" She was my fairy godmother and the only friend I ever had. People avoided me, pretended I didn't exist, until I would say or do something dorky. That was all the time. Then, they called me names. I'd heard them all, more times than I could count. And I liked to count. I would time things to arrive with the bus and would run home, the minute I got off. The rowdy boys sat at the back of the bus. I sat right behind the driver, one leg curled beneath my butt, so I could bounce. Bouncing was one of the dorky things I did, but I couldn't help it. It was my *stim.* That's what doctors called it — short for self-stimulation, but not **that** kind of self-stimulation. Between me and the rowdy boys, was a sea of empty seats and island of girls.

On the twenty-seventh day of school, Pee's cloak of invisibility stopped working. One of the Desert Rats plopped beside me. He had stained and dirty Keds with a loose sole flapping beneath his toes. I notice shoes. I can tell a lot about a person from shoes. I don't like to look at faces. They look back and that hurts. Under his mop of red hair were freckles thicker than a bag of red hots. "If you're livin' in the 'hood, might as well join our gang."

I froze in horror, realizing I wasn't invisible.

"I'm Scotty, and that's my house." He pointed to the trailer nearest the bus stop. "I'm in eighth grade. Stud says you're in his social studies class. Joey, right?"

That's me, Joey, nicknamed after a baby kangaroo 'cause I bounce.

I noticed dirt beneath his fingernails. He hadn't washed in a month and he extended that dirty hand. "Glad to meet you, Joey." Handshakes are part of the guy code. But, touching that revolting hand was *groatable.* Groat was the word I invented to describe a sound I made — a cross between a train horn and buzz saw. I couldn't help groats. They would rise up from deep inside and spill out like the horn ending a basketball game. When he grabbed my hand, the groat escaped. It sounded when an electric shock shot through my hand and up my arm. My groat became a scream.

Scotty had an electric gizmo in his palm. "Don't be a pussy. It's a capacitor. Come on and meet the boys." He pulled my arm down the aisle. I wished I were Stretch Armstrong to avoid going. Doe-eyed girls watched him tug me to my fate.

"Guys, this's Joey. That's Stud."

From class, I recognized the steel-toed Army brogans, spiky blond hair, and a neck as thick as my thigh. It was obvious why they called him Stud. Girls swooned over his muscles.

"All the Rats got nicknames," Stud said.

"That's Kipper." Scotty pointed to a boy with rattlesnake cowboy boots and inky hair.

"Hola, Joey. I'm in Séptimo grade."

"Kipper?" I asked.

"I comer sardines," he explained.

That puzzled me. "Sardines aren't kippers. Kippers are herrings."

"Tell these chicos," Kipper shrugged.

A short boy, without shoes, sitting on Kipper's seat said, "I'm Winkle, sixth-grade. Kipper speaks Spanish 'cause he's a Mexican from Guadalajara in Jalisco, where the j sounds like an h."

"Winkle is shord fer Periwinkle," a tall and skinny boy in Converse shoes explained. "His mudder dyed his undies."

"On purpose?"

"No," Winkle answered. "She washed them after tie-dying my sister's play costume."

"Why wear them?" I asked.

"Too poor for new ones. 'Sides, they're my signature now. Wanna see?"

Winkle lifted the waistband of his tighty-whity briefs above his jeans. They were lavender, as advertised. Stud grabbed the waistband and pulled it into a wedgie.

Winkle laughed and rearranged his undies. "Got skid marks, now."

Converse shoe boy shook my hand. "I'm Rufus. Eighth grade." He had a ruddy brown complexion, raven-colored Mohawk, and crooked teeth between high cheekbones and a pointed chin. He looked like they'd held him back several years.

"Rufus is Pima Indian," Winkle added. "He 'scaped the reservation. He scalps guys."

Rufus pulled a huge switchblade from his jeans pocket, flicked it open, and grabbed my hair. My eyes bugged out and I about pissed my pants. "They let you take that to school?"

"Dey got no choice. I gut dem like a catz fish."

The smallest, a black boy with an afro, said, "Rufus rhymes with doofus."

"Iz haint very smard." Rufus shrugged. "Did Scotty shock youz? He'll zap youz ebery time."

When I nodded, Stud laughed. "We only keep Scotty 'round to fix our walkie-talkies."

"Eat shit," Scotty said. "I'm Lieutenant of the Desert Rats." He pointed to the black boy who wore brown Sperry Top-Siders, Khaki Dockers, and had a 'fro pick stuck over his Dumbo-sized right ear. "That's Bobby. He's in sixth."

"So, is Robert his real name?" I asked.

"If you knew my real name, I'd have to kill you," Bobby said.

"At first his nick was Booby cause he's always hangin' on his ma's tits," Scotty said. "She dresses him."

"Does not!" Bobby objected in a snotty whine.

"Mama's tits are muy grande," Kipper said.

"Like 52 triple D's," Stud added.

"Bazookas." Scotty illustrated by putting his fists beneath his t-shirt.

Winkle laughed. "One time, I yelled across the playground, 'Hey, Booby.' Teacher didn't like that, so we changed it to Bobby. You won't believe it, but he's wearing Ninja Turtle Underoos."

"Am not!" Bobby whined as the gang laughed.

"Dare you to prove it, Bobby," Winkle challenged.

"Drop 'um," Rufus said. "Dats a dare."

"Scotty, girls are on the bus," Bobby whined.

"They won't see nothing," Winkle said.

Kipper held his thumb and index finger an inch apart. "Es muy poco."

"Want me to pants him?" Stud volunteered.

Bobby dropped his Dockers. "See. Good enough?"

The guys laughed because they *were* Underoos. Bobby laughed too. I realized teasing could be friendly, not mean-spirited. I laughed. There is one hell of a big difference between laughing with and laughing at. I never realized prepositions were so powerful.

Scotty dropped something into Bobby's underwear, as he pulled up his pants.

"Waid fer id," Rufus whispered.

When Bobby sat, he jumped several feet high. "Damn it, Scotty! That hurt!" He pulled out a capacitor.

"Shock youz tiny Vienna sausage inda growin'," Rufus teased.

I'd been teased mercilessly for most of my life. But this banter was different. Everyone smiled and laughed. I didn't need a groat. I was happy to not be invisible. I wanted to know more.

"You must be Scott," I said.

"Wrong," Winkle said. "Scotty wore his sister's plaid skirt for Halloween."

"It was a kilt. I went commando like a real Scot," Scotty said.

"I'm Joey, like a baby kangaroo," I said.

"Dat why youz a bouncin' all da time?" Rufus asked.

"I'd nickname you Tigger," Winkle suggested. "My lil' bro likes *Winnie the Pooh*."

I stared at him. "Joey, like a baby kangaroo."

"Fair nuff," Rufus said.

"Joey es," Kipper said.

"Joey, got wheels?" Scotty asked.

"What?"

"A 'cycle or dirt bike?" Stud rephrased. "Every Desert Rat has wheels 'sept for Bobby. I've gotta Volkswagen Beetle that Rufus and my bro fixed. We torched off the top so it's like a convertible."

"Whadda youz mean hepped? I did mostda work." Rufus claimed.

"Rufus rides a minibike," Scotty said. "Like a scarecrow flying on a banana seat."

"Tote Goat for me," Winkle said. "Scotty has a smoking Yamaha, and Kipper rides his dad's Harley chopper."

"I … I … I'm too young to drive" I used to have a bad stutter because my mind ran a thousand miles away from my mouth. Years of speech therapy corrected it, but it still comes out when I'm stressed.

"All the Rats is too young, 'cept Rufus," Scotty said. "No one needs a license in the desert."

"Youz uncle hadda jeep," Rufus said. "Axe him to led youz run it."

"I don't figure he will." Mom and I had recently moved in with Uncle Timmy 'cause money ran out. On the carport, he had a 1942 Willy's Jeep he'd restored from World War II. The thought of asking was daunting.

"No harm in askin'," Stud said.

"Where'd you get the name Desert Rats?" I asked them.

Winkle answered. "Old TV show called *Rat Patrol* about an American jeep crew in the North Africa desert during World War II. Scotty's dad has a box set of the series on DVD. You must watch it."

"So, I'm part of the Desert Rats?" I asked in disbelief.

"Not so fast. You have to pass initiation." Scotty answered.

As I trotted home, I soared. I had friends and getting them wasn't so hard. But I fretted about the initiation. To have friends, I'd do anything. It was my One Most Important Thing. And, I wanted to drive, as they did, so much …I could just imagine the desert wind burning my face.

After Mom left for work, I curled up on the couch beside Uncle Timmy and watched football. I mustered courage. The Sun Devils made a good play, and he hooted.

Pee giggled. *Joey, this's your chance.*

"Uncle Timmy, the trailer park boys have motorcycles and dirt bikes they ride in the desert. Mom doesn't have money to buy me one. Do you think I could drive your Jeep?"

He pulled my head into his lap, so I looked right up at him. "Are you making friends?"

"I hope so."

"Know how to drive?"

"Could you teach me?"

He tousled my hair. I could put up with some tousling. Hell, if it got me what I wanted, I'd let him pet me for hours.

"What would your mother say?"

"Does she have to know? Couldn't it be between us guys?" I looked into his eyes, although it was hard. Adults liked eye contact.

"Let's go." He smiled.

I hugged him, and I don't give hugs often. I climbed into the passenger bucket seat, not standard on old Jeeps, and buckled my seatbelt.

"See the big bar overhead? That's the roll cage. It'll keep you safe if the Jeep rolls, as long as you have your seat belt buckled."

"Don't worry, Uncle Timmy, seat belt buckling is Rule #15." In an hour, I knew how to drive the jeep, including shifting the gears.

The next afternoon, Uncle Timmy asked, "Sis, why don't we catch burgers over at the root beer stand before you go to work?"

"That would be fine," Mom answered.

"I want to shake cobwebs off the Jeep. Mind a bumpy ride?"

"Sounds like fun," Mom said.

He winked at me. "I'll have Joey pull it around."

"Joey?" Mom's voice shot to high soprano.

"Don't sell the kid short."

I was flying high when I stopped the Jeep in the yard near the front door. Mom paused. Uncle Timmy jumped into the back and left me at the wheel. "Climb in Sis, Joey's driving."

"Joey?" She hesitated but took a seat.

As I roared the jeep into the desert, two motorcycles pulled in front of us, as if they were cops escorting a dignitary. Soon, the 'meep, meep, meep' sound of a VW Beetle's horn came up behind us, flanked by a minibike and tote goat paralleling it in the sand.

"Mom, these are my new friends."

At the root beer stand, Uncle Timmy bought burgers, fries, and root beers for everyone, including the Desert Rats. We ate on the patio under beach umbrellas. I introduced my new friends to Mom and Uncle Timmy. Mom didn't control her look of surprise while Uncle Timmy shook their hands.

As I drove home, Mom touched my elbow. "I'm glad you're making friends. Buddies are important."

"It was easy, Mom. They wanted to be my friend." After I said this, I wondered if it had been as easy as I thought. I'd had to endure a dirty handshake and shock from a capacitor. And, the initiation loomed. Hope I could I endure whatever was coming.

That Saturday was a scorcher. I heard a cacophony of loud engines outside. I ran out to meet the Desert Rats.

"Ready for your initiation?" Stud asked over the torched-off top of his Beetle.

The thought made me want to groat. Unknown things aren't easy for me. I need an ordered schedule and familiar things to do. I always wear my Monday shirt on Monday. We have spaghetti on Thursday. Popcorn with an HBO movie on Friday night. Offering myself for whatever shenanigan the Desert Rats planned wasn't going to be easy. I had to convince myself it was my One Most Important Thing.

I climbed into the Beetle's backseat beside Bobby. I watched Pee hover over the driveway. *You're coming, too. Aren't you?*

She shook her head. *This's just for boys.*

Stud followed the motorcycles into the desert. We bounced across the banks of a wide ditch and sped over the sand. Tall saguaros pointed toward the sky and creosote bushes browned in the hot sun. I thought about rattlesnakes and what I'd have to do for the initiation.

"Bobby, what do I have to do?" I asked.

"Jump off a cliff into the river, naked."

"Did you?"

"Yeah."

Stud chuckled. "Bobby, tell the truth or I will."

Bobby frowned. "OK. I chickened out. They stripped me and tossed me off the ledge."

Stud laughed. "You should've heard him whine, snivel and cry." Stud's voice turned falsetto. "No. Please. I'll tell my mommy."

I laughed. "You were that much of a pussy?" I secretly hoped to do better.

We followed desert trails north into a river valley and parked beneath cottonwood trees. Noontime sun dappled through the shade.

"This is the Salt River and one of our favorite swimming holes," Stud said.

Scotty warned, "Hope you're not a prude 'cause we skinny dip."

As I walked to the river, I saw dozens of people riding inner tubes and rafts — kids, mothers, teenaged girls, and guys drinking beer out of floating ice chests. "You skinny dip in front of all these people?"

"Scared?" Rufus teased.

"He'll pop a boner," Kipper suggested.

With defiance, I pulled off my shirt and unzipped my shorts.

Winkle stopped me. "Whoa! Silly, not yet, not here — at the cliffs."

"Let's go." I wanted to get past the ordeal.

We hiked to a bridge, crossed the highway, and followed a trail half-a-mile upriver. I was at the top of a hundred-foot cliff. It wasn't sheer, instead, eroded ledges jutted out like unevenly stacked dinner plates. I saw kids on a ledge below.

"I'm not jumping from here," I said. "It's suicide."

Scotty shrugged and laughed. "Jump out far enough to clear."

I looked down again. I never thought I had a fear of heights, but this brought a panicked groat from my mouth. Dizziness made me teeter at the edge. I stuttered a few words. "I c … c … can't j … j … jump." A groat exploded from my mouth. Defeated, I turned from the cliff and sat.

"Why are you making a funny noise?" Winkle asked.

"That's my g … g … groat. I h … have a … autism." I cried.

"Audism?" Rufus said as if it were the strangest word in the world.

"What the hell is that?" Scotty asked.

I felt frustrated at having to out myself. Autism was a secret I seldom shared. "My brain is different from yours," I tried to explain.

"Mine is, too," Stud admitted. "I can't read for shit. Some of the letters turn backwards and dance."

I expected the Rats to ditch me in the desert. The humiliation of groating and admitting my autism was worse than plunging to my death. I stood there on the ledge, jerked off my shorts and underwear in less than a second, and threw myself off the cliff, eyes closed. I was willing to risk death to have friends. I waited for the crash at the cliff's bottom. Oddly, I wasn't falling. Instead, someone held me. I opened my eyes.

Stud had me wrapped in his arms. "Damn! You have brass balls to try that jump."

I struggled against Stud. "Let me jump!" I wanted friends more than anything.

"We don't jump from here," Winkle said. "This was just to scare you."

"You're the first one brave enough to try it," Scotty admitted with a smile. "We'll go down to the ledge."

Winkle handed me my shorts, and I stepped into them commando, sticking my underwear into my pocket.

"Guys who jump here hit da ground 'stead a water," Rufus said. "All dey make is news."

My eyes grew wide and the boys laughed at my reaction. I worked to slow my heart as we descended to about thirty feet above the water. Erosion had hollowed out a bowl in the cliff. People were there, and some climbed toward it. A massive boulder sat in the water below. It was deadly. I watched a few jumpers aim beside it and I realized it wouldn't be a leap of death.

"Go on," Scotty said. "Pull off your shorts and jump."

I got shy about getting naked because fifty tubers were in the water below. "You already saw me naked. No need to do it again."

"It da rule," Rufus said.

"What are you worried about?" Stud asked.

"The girls will salute when they see your dick flapping in the wind." Winkle laughed.

I pulled off my shorts. The nearby people jeered and laughed. That made the tubers catch my nakedness and add to the roar. Though I wanted to cover myself, I stepped to the edge, waving my shorts overhead like a lasso. An incredible rush hit me as my back foot left the rock.

I straightened out mid-air, wanting to enter feet first. An eternity passed in those three seconds before I plunged into the river. The water rushed over my body and pushed up my nose. I fought to the surface. "Woo-hoo! That was fantastic!" I yelled.

I'd lost my shorts in the jump, but they soon bobbed up in the current. I swam to catch them hold of them. I couldn't find my underwear. The cool water on my body felt wonderful. Kipper was right. A boner popped, and I didn't give a shit. I let the current carry me downstream to the bridge, where I swam to the river bank, scampered out, and stepped into my soggy shorts. I sat on the bridge railing and watched other jumpers and the tubers float beneath me.

Within several minutes, the Desert Rats came, returning from the trail we'd hiked. We walked back to our wheels. Under the cottonwoods, we swam, roughhousing and splashing all afternoon. At twilight, we headed south.

"Next, you'll visit our secret hideout," Stud said.

It was a quarter-mile into the desert from the trailer park, near enough you could see cars on the highway if you looked between slats of the pallets that were its walls. They still bore the markings of the nearby Safeway. The hideout was in the middle of a deep wash where Palo Verde trees grew tall. Thrown-away furniture — a ratty red couch, card table chairs, a wooden drop-leaf table, a double-bed mattress — filled the hideout.

Scotty lit a Coleman lantern. "You must check it for snakes and scorpions."

Rufus poked around the furniture with a broom handle and flipped couch cushions.

"Now you're one of us," Scotty said.

"Really?" I couldn't believe anyone would want to be my friend. Nobody ever had. "Despite my problem?"

"We've all got problems," Scotty laughed. "My dad's disabled and on Social Security."

"My dad had a heart attack," Bobby added.

"It was an ugly divorce," Winkle winced. "My sister and brother come from a different dad and he was a mean cuss."

"I'm illegal," Kipper smirked. "Just me and Pancho here, mi familia is still in Mexico."

"My dad's in jail and Mom tossed me out," Rufus said. "I live with Mormon missionaries."

"La pandilla de chicos rotos," Kipper smiled.

"The gang of broken boys," Scotty translated.

"That's the Desert Rats," Winkle said.

We talked until night deepened and the desert cooled. I realized I had much to learn from friends. For the first time, I felt like I'd found a home.

Author's Bio:

Gary Kidney writes from Pearland, TX. He holds a Master of Fine Arts degree in creative writing from Albertus Magnus College in New Haven, CT. His publications include two other short stories. "I Have a Fairy Godmother" was published in The Furious Gazelle in November 2016. That story was a finalist in the fiction competition for Pen2Paper 2017 where writing focused on disabilities. "College Visit" was published in The Mighty Line in January 2019. That story was an honorable mention in the 13th Annual Writer's Digest Popular Fiction Awards. Gary is currently seeking an agent for several completed books.

One Between

By Sarah Kaminski

You were easy. There were all the usual bits—the sickness and the exhaustion—but you were still so easy. Only a few weeks off birth control, and then you existed.

That night, we got so drunk, I'd joke. Your father would roll his eyes, but I knew the truth. I felt the change almost immediately. I threw up six weeks later. One moment, I sat in a classroom; the next, I raced along unfamiliar hallways, searching and failing to find a bathroom, until it all came bubbling up pink and orange and sour. I stained the pale blue walls.

I could tell you were a boy before my first ultrasound. You flattened me. You made my heart race and my stomach churn. You left me weak and helpless. You had to be a boy. A girl wouldn't be so cruel.

"He looks like a rabbit," I said. White blobs on black background.

"He's not."

"How big is he?" I asked.

"The size of a walnut." The nurse sounded bored.

I couldn't believe that something so small could wreak such havoc, but you did. For forty-one weeks, you owned my body, inhabited it, my little parasite. You were born with thick black hair, purplish-red skin, nearly nine pounds. I threw up an hour before you crowned. I labored for thirty-one hours, but pushed only twice. Then there you were. Perfection. I couldn't keep my eyes off of you. I begged to hold you, even before the nurses cleaned you off.

Nobody warns you about the depth of love you will have for your child. When they took you away to clean the blood from your hair and the mucus from your eyes, I couldn't bear to be separated from you. It hurt to have you near, yet outside my grasp.

I grew terrified of ever leaving your side. On the second day, when I couldn't stand not having showered, I dared to take you to the nursery for half an hour, a mere thirty minutes—an eternity. When my milk came in, my breasts swelled to twice their size, hard and painful. The nurses smiled and called me lucky to have a good supply, but you wouldn't latch and the pain grew worse. I worried you might starve, that my body would fail you. When you screamed with hunger, I cried as well.

I suffered a year's worth of soaked-through shirts, dry cracked nipples, painful bites of razor-sharp teeth just poking through the gums, grabs and pinches with viselike nails, endless pumping—reducing myself to a cow for your benefit. I felt only pride that my body had created life—your home, your nourishment, and your playground.

—

You were young, only two years old; do you remember when we sat with you on the couch and wrapped arms around your shoulders and told you you'd be a big brother soon? You won't remember some parts. I know that. You were asleep when I presented the peed-on stick and gleefully announced, "This one will be easy, because we've done it once before."

You weren't there when the sonogram technician struggled for half an hour before saying, in her well-practiced voice, "There's no heartbeat. I'm sorry."

Stupid me, I asked, "What does that mean?"

You were just a toddler and wouldn't understand. You weren't there for the painful lunch, when your daddy and I debated what to do. Wait it out? Take the medications to "jump start" the natural process? Or D&C? Have two letters ever been so hateful?

"I want to wait," I said over uneaten pasta. "I want to let it happen naturally."

I wanted to hold on to the hope that it was all a mistake, that my second baby was still alive. The joke, the real horror, was that the ultrasound of death looked more human than yours ever had. There had been no morning sickness. None of the heart-racing dizziness followed by a mad rush to the toilet that I'd known with you.

"It must be a girl," my mother had joked.

"I hope," I replied, already dreaming of pink tutus, and dance slippers, wedding dresses and secrets over ice cream: a lifetime of mother-daughter moments that I would eventually never have.

As my eldest, you have always been such a boy, all dirt and toy guns, climbing, jumping, attacking. Two years old and you used my body like a jungle gym. Taking running leaps into my lap when I stretched out on the couch.

"You can't jump on Mommy's tummy," your father warned. First in calm sweet tones, and then more sternly, "Stop!" I curled around my stomach to protect the life inside. Impossible to know when that heart formed at eight weeks, stopped cold. Had it never started?

—

The bleeding began while your father was out of town, leaving you and me alone. We were driving home. I wore a pad, preemptive protection, but it wasn't enough. I felt it begin, hot liquid and more gushing between my legs, while I sat helpless at a red light. You babbled in the backseat and I filled the spaces with empty affirmatives.

"Uh huh."

"Wow!"

"That's cool!"

Mother's perfect *not-listening* early on.

I drove home soaked in my own blood, and when I climbed gingerly from the car, I felt gelatinous substance squish between my legs, warmth dribble down my thighs. Only two, you begged to be carried inside, and I couldn't bring myself to do it. You started crying, and I screamed.

"Shut up!" Terrible mother. "Just shut the fuck up!"

You did, but that look in your eyes. Another death on my hands.

You shrieked in the living room, while I raced to the bathroom and peeled soaked jeans off my body. I sat on the toilet and scrubbed my legs and sobbed while life poured out. I listened to you scream in the room down the hall, filling every inch of the house and I did nothing to soothe you.

Instead, I forced myself to look at the mess in my underwear: the pad that overflowed in less than an hour, the dark red that oozed off the sides, the tissue like cherry cola Jell-O at a Fourth of July picnic, and in the center of it all, the white, shrimp-like thing curled and dead.

Tiny little thing.

I stuffed it into a black trash bag, a murderer disposing of the fetus. I hid the evidence. Do you remember moving in with Grandma for a week? Do you remember how Mommy slept on the couch all day, getting up only to hide in the bathroom? Do you remember Grandma taking over the lunches and dinners, the bedtime stories, and the games? Do you remember how I couldn't bring myself to look at you, except with hurt and anger at my loss, our family's loss?

Nobody warns you about the depth of hatred you will have for your own child. Will your first memory be of me screaming, kicking the wall in anger, sobbing on the floor? When you are grown, will you remember when Mommy lost control? Have I damaged our relationship forever?

"What if it was *his* fault?" I whispered to your father, while you slept.

"Don't say that."

"I need to know what I did wrong."

"You didn't do anything wrong."

Then why was I being punished? I had once felt so proud of my body for creating life; now I hated it for destroying it.

—

Months passed of trying for a third time, waiting, and failing. When the test finally read positive again, two pink lines on a white background, I felt only fear. No giddy bouncing of my knee, as I waited in the doctor's office for the sonogram. Only my breath held anxiously, until the technician smiled and said, "There's the heartbeat."

Life.

Later, when your new brother was born, the past seemed forgiven.

"Baby brother," you crooned as you pat his downy red hair. His existence is your memory and my miracle. But will you remember the one that came between?

MAIA'S CALL

By Ed Burke

Wind - whipped snow flew across the field. Standing at the window, I felt the gale force winds rake Maia's cabin. Stillness inside. The only sound came from the woodstove; settling embers. Five days ago I had parked the rented Corolla in the rutted drive, which ended at Carlisle, a hilltop in Vermont.

In the previous week, I had no idea I would be here, or what would be waiting for me. The Northeast was a vague notion in my head when Maia had called. I knew something about Vermont from what Maia had written me years ago: about swimming holes and frozen pipes, deer in the fields and berry picking. She had told me about her neighbors and the man she lived with. About remote solitude. About her baby son Luke, born five years ago, or so. She had sent me a picture of the pink little newborn squinting at the world. In the years that followed, she had sent photos and brief notes from the cabin where I now stood. I had sent bits of news back to her from San Francisco. It had been about two years since I had last heard from her.

It had been so long since we had talked, I was thrilled to hear her voice on that fateful evening when she called. She said she had to make it quick, that we could catch up later. I asked where she was staying, thinking she might be in San Francisco visiting. She answered she was in Vermont. She added, "I'm dying, Tom. I'd like to see you. Can you do that?" Her voice trembled.

I didn't hesitate, "Of course."

"Thank you." Then she added, "I have end stage leukemia. I don't want to talk about it over the phone."

I told her I didn't either, and that I'd leave the next day. She said she loved me. I didn't realize it, but I was crying when I told her I loved her too. One of us hung up first. I was alone in the kitchen with the weak echo of her voice in my head.

Jeffrey, my husband, came into the room, "Who was on the phone?"

"It was Maia. She says she's dying. I need to go see her."

Jeffrey stepped forward, as I knew he would. He cupped my face in his hand and brushed my cheek with his thumb.

"I need to go."

"Of course you do." He brushed my cheek again.

I wasn't able to hold any memories of Maia, as I prepared for the trip. She was a wisp blown in from the past. I grasped at things I knew I should have recalled, but she kept vanishing. The years we had spent together in California were like they had never happened, no matter how hard I tried to conjure an occasion or a feeling. Each effort to recall her was deterred by a shadowed voice: *she's dying.*

*

I arrived in Boston just before noon and called Jeffrey to let him know I had arrived safely, and that I loved him. As we spoke, I gazed out of the terminal windows. It was my first time east. A cold March sky weighed down on the city. People hunched against the gray, even those inside. Some intuitive part of me took control from the directions my phone was giving, and I escaped the airport and flew through the sullen city, hitting all the turns I needed. Boston fell behind and I was on the Massachusetts Turnpike.

Hills, covered with bare trees, rolled by under the leaden sky, broken up occasionally by some low, flat commercial buildings or housing tracts. The scenery seemed to keep repeating on some tired treadmill. Clouds began to spit snow. I remembered her smile when we had first met at a party, summer twilight outside Petaluma. Her eyes glowed. I loved her then, immediately. I remembered thinking: *her soul must shine.* The recollection scattered. Hills surrounded me again. I thought, *do her eyes still shine?* Her deep brown eyes. *She's dying.*

Full memories surfaced in detail as I drove: the two of us touching, making love, and arguing. Several meals: a breakfast of chorizo and eggs in sunshine, dinner at the apartment— shrimp scampi by candlelight. I remembered her beside me in bed, waiting for an explanation. *She's dying.* I tried pushing these memories aside, but couldn't. The last night I had spent with her, I shifted my eyes to the ceiling. She had asked me repetitively, "So, do you love him?"

I now heard those same words again, as if she were sitting in the car beside me. I said aloud, as I did eight years ago, the only answer I could give: "Yes." I felt sick to my stomach as I did then, revisiting the bitter heartbreak I had caused her. I crossed into Vermont. The mountains along the interstate darkened with evergreens, snow flew at my windshield.

I remembered when Maia said goodbye, months after the night I had told her about Jeffrey outside my apartment — her car packed. She was leaving San Francisco, moving to New Mexico. She had a friend there. Standing by her car, she said she loved me, still. I loved her, but didn't say it. It was different now. We swore we'd keep in touch. I heard those promises again, as clear as yesterday. Loose promises.

No, we kept our promises. As busy as life got, we kept in touch. I had moved in with Jeffrey and enrolled in graduate school for engineering. Maia was making jewelry in Santa Fe. I was twenty - five, she was twenty - seven. She sent me a postcard to tell me she was happy there. I smiled when I got the card, thinking of her dancing eyes. Over the next few years, I'd get an occasional note on postcards, menus, lavender writing paper, scratch pad paper from Flagstaff; Tulsa; Athens; Georgia; Pittsburgh; Glover, Vermont. She'd tell me how she liked working at a daycare, picking apples, harvesting lettuce, serving food at a co-operative, serving food at a diner, serving food at a Denny's — telling me how she loved or hated the people she was hanging out with, the picnics they went on, the music they played. How the places she lived in were crowded: cold, grungy, sunny, spacious farms, forests, slums. I'd write back about my studies and the city. I didn't see our old friends much, after I moved in with Jeffrey, but I'd mention who I'd run into. I had new friends. They were older, many involved, one way or another, with Jeffrey's architectural firm. I'd tell Maia about some of the obnoxious things they did. I didn't get into much detail about my life, nor tell her how content I was with Jeffrey, because I didn't want to hurt her feelings. My happiness felt unfair. I must have told her somehow, because she had written she was glad for me.

The snow fell hard against the windshield, blanketing the car in white. I slowed down. I didn't sense happiness or love in most of Maia's notes, despite what the words stated, although she was crazy in love for a while with a man named Doug. They had moved to Vermont and had a son, Luke. The letter she sent me with the first baby pictures was truly joyful. In her later notes, with pictures of Luke growing up, she described her life as good, but I knew there was much she wasn't telling me. Then, three years ago the letters stopped, and Maia faded away.

*

I found her cabin at the end of a rutted drive, on top of a remote hill. I arrived in the failing last light of evening, the snow squall an hour behind me. A woman greeted me at the door: a thin, young woman wearing jeans and a faded, oversized Disney World sweatshirt. Her limp, light brown hair was loosely tied back. She introduced herself as Rita, Doug's sister. She was just leaving. Standing at the door, she said it was nice to meet me. "I'll be back sometime towards supper tomorrow." She said over her shoulder. I looked past Rita, saw Maia, barely visible, in a hospital bed half way across the poorly lit room. I entered the cabin.

When the front door closed behind Rita, a sudden quiet overwhelmed me. I listened to the pickup truck start up. I peered into the gloom and noticed one large room with a door opened to a small bathroom, and another door which seemed shut. I figured the closed door led to an unused bedroom. A kitchen sink, range and an old refrigerator lined the far wall. A small round table stood in the near corner of the room. It was covered with papers, books and an ashtray. Two wooden chairs were placed at the table. A faded, overstuffed easy chair was set by the woodstove, where stood an upright lamp beside the chair and paperbacks on the floor. I glanced up at the rough beams, dark with age, running the width of the cabin ceiling twelve feet above, and at the ash-smudged plaster between these beams. The woodstove chuffed smoke from the misfit door.

Maia waited.

Still standing by the front door, I asked, "How long have you lived here?"

"Five years. Since we arrived in Vermont." Her voice was weak, soft.

I shuddered at the thought of Maia being in this place for so long. I studied her lying in that monstrous bed, in that one large room, studied her lined face.

Her eyes shone on me. "It's good to see you Tom. I'm glad you're here."

I felt the worn pine boards beneath my feet dissolve and I was falling, surrounded by a blank sky that gave me no clue as to what would be. But her eyes held mine.

Without thinking I asked, "Why?"

I stepped forward and came within a few feet from her. The bed, with its institutional smell and stern metal frame, served as a stronghold. It held Maia, beneath her magenta –purple and rose crocheted afghan. Her birdwing shoulders showed through her faded t - shirt. Her skull, with its scattered tufts of mouse brown hair, was perched on her stem-thin neck.

She smiled, slightly, "Can you put water for some tea?"

"Sure." I went to her bedside and put my hand over one of her cold hands resting on the afghan.

At the stained sink, I focused on filling the kettle I found on the range. I couldn't do anything more. Maia didn't speak. With my back to her, I imagined she was watching me. *She's dying.* I peered out the window above the sink, past a rangy spider plant on the window shelf, and saw a large doe and her fawn nibbling bark in a stand of saplings, halfway across the field beyond the cabin. The creatures stretched their tawny necks in the last light of dusk. This is what Maia saw from her sink. A new piece of her fit in my mind. The kettle clanged against the iron burner ring. The deer pricked their ears. I felt Maia jolt.

"If the flame doesn't catch, there's matches on the shelf over the stove." She said.

The gas lit after a couple clicks, a blue flame spread beneath the kettle. I asked where the tea was, and found: Lipton orange pekoe, Darjeeling, a couple boxes of Celestial Seasonings, chamomile. She preferred chamomile with honey. When I turned, I noticed her watching me. She reached for a handle on the side of the bed and pressed a button. The head of the bed tilted upright. "That's better. This way I can keep an eye on you." She brightened.

I tossed back I was there to steal her honey. I noticed her bedside table was cluttered: a mug, a glass with an inch of water, a paperback, a box of Kleenex and some wadded tissues. I asked, "Can I clear some of this away?"

She shut her eyes. "Yes, thanks."

She's in pain! Her agony surged through me as I cleared a spot for tea. I lifted the paperback, *Love Medicine*, from the table, "Great book."

She smiled crookedly, "I know. You gave it to me."

I remembered — the day, the bookstore, the rain, and the coffee later as we read to each other. San Francisco, alive together.

Her eyes sparked, "I've read just about all of Louise Erdrich since then." She rubbed the afghan where it draped next to her hip, "She's amazing." Then, she shut her eyes.

The kettle whistled and I realized I was crying. With two steaming mugs placed on the bedside table, the tea's aroma filled the space between us. I brought a rickety Windsor chair over so Maia didn't have to tilt her head to see me. Before I sat down, she asked me to put another log in the stove and apologized for the poor heat, "It's pretty green. I didn't quite get it together to get seasoned wood this year." She shut her eyes, "His folks helped me get what wood I've got."

As I poked the coals to life, I asked, "Doug's folks?"

"Yes. They've been a lot of help through all this. He has a brother, three sisters, a boatload of cousins. His parents, they're still around. Everybody helping out. Well mostly everybody. His sisters bring me food. Take my wash. Rita — who you met — she watches Luke. He's there now, with her kids like most of the time, but he does see me almost every day..."

Her breath was thin, drawing in air through her teeth. I touched her hand. I wanted to ask why she was in this cabin-shack on the side of this fucking mountain. I pulled my hand back — I didn't want her to feel what I was thinking. "How's the tea?"

She raise the mug, "Still hot."

I followed the movement of her hand, "What's happening, Maia?"

She leaned back, sank into the pillow, shut her eyes, "Leukemia. End stage."

"Why did you call me?"

"I needed someone here who loved me."

I corrected her, "Who loves you."

"I'm scared."

"It will be alright." I managed to say, then bowed my head.

"Are you happy?" She asked after a long pause.

"Yes."

"Tell me about Jeffrey." She smiled in a way that gave me permission.

My heart swelled in that instant. I wanted to be close to Maia when I told her what he meant to me. "Can I lie there with you?"

Maia turned her head slightly, opened her eyes, "I'd like that." She shut her eyes again, "There are a couple throw pillows on the easy chair, and another afghan. Night's falling, it gets cold."

My eyes wandered out the windows into the black beyond the cabin's shelter. I needed to hold Maia. I needed the distance between us to disappear. I wanted us to meld into something else. I got beneath the covers with her, wearing everything except my shoes. We shut our eyes and talked. We held hands beneath the covers. We sipped some tea. We listened to years and lives pass by. Dreams, hopes, hardship and joy spun between us.

She told me how I had devastated her. She said it was like I tore her heart from her chest. She said she didn't understand, that she thought we were perfect together. She had had no time or chance to prepare herself. She asked me how it happened that I could fall in love with someone else, with Jeffrey. I told her I couldn't have imagined it happening, but it did. I met him and some wild horse inside me I'd never known, yet suspected, kicked down the gates and galloped breakneck away with me. It was all I could do to hang on, and I knew I wanted it to never end.

"And what about me?"

How could I answer? She was almost nothing compared to that ferocious passion. I tried. I told her it was something amazing that I had to have. I explained that I knew I had hurt her then, but I was so obsessed with Jeffrey, there was no room for empathy. In her hospital bed I tried to right that wrong as best I could, "I'm sorry."

She turned away. The cabin creaked in the wind. She squeezed my hand, "You love him very much."

"I do."

She took a sip of the lukewarm tea, "I was a mess, you know. I felt like my entire life had been sucked out of me. I don't remember you moving out. I spent those weeks at Sheila's, crashed on her couch. We'd go out. Get drunk, or not. Pick up a guy, or not. It didn't matter. Nothing mattered. I couldn't handle it at all. I'm glad we didn't run into each other then. I don't know what I would have done, but it probably would have been ugly. Maybe I should have made you tell me why you didn't love me, but I couldn't." She paused then, "There was nothing for me in San Francisco, so I took off. Sheila mentioned a friend of hers in Santa Fe and I was gone a week later. At least Santa Fe was different. Everything was new so I had to pull my shit together. The jewelry gig was okay, no money of course. It didn't matter. I got together with a guy, Eric, pretty full of himself in that alpha leftie kind of way. He dumped me before I knew it. I watched him plow through one hippie chick after another. It was pretty disgusting. Then I kind of withdrew, watched the bullshit, copped an attitude I guess. I made my jewelry, hung out, that was about it. After a while I headed to Flagstaff, did farm labor with Sheila's friend, who hated the Santa Fe thing too. We busted hump, lived clean. I moved on to the next gig when I wanted a change. Kept doing that. Hooked up with a couple guys who turned out to be assholes almost immediately. I'd put up with their crap until I'd had enough. Same shit, different day." Maia's whisper stopped, she sipped some tea. She asked, "Are you okay with this? I'm rambling."

I told her it was alright, then I asked her how she had met Doug. Maia put her mug down, settled back into her pillows. I tucked the blanket back over her shoulder.

She started, stronger, "Doug was different. I met him when I was waiting tables at a Denny's in Pittsburgh. He liked my morning glory tattoo." She smiled at this. "Which was cool because I was really proud of it. Right then he asked me out. I said yeah, okay, maybe coffee sometime. He said fine. Just like that."

"Just like that?"

"Yeah, I was liking him more and more, so that by the end of his meal, I was thinking I could go for this guy. He was wearing work clothes, you know jeans and a flannel shirt. He worked at a place that made prefab housing. He hated it, said he'd rather be building houses on site, but it was steady work. His brother got him the job after he'd been laid off from some factory in Vermont. It was steady pay he said, so no reason to complain." She paused again, then slowly resumed her story. "He told me all this over that first cup of coffee at this place that we both liked. He was good looking, smelled good, and had a bad boy twinkle in his blue eyes. He was different from the scamming drifters out there. So we went out." Her eyes were distant in thought when she spoke. "He didn't try to get me in bed that first night, but we knew where things were headed. Next date I had him over to my place and the rest, as they say, is history. It was great. He treated me right, and not just when we were alone. In front of his friends, too. He was great in bed. He paid for my drinks, made me laugh. We were having fun, that's all I know."

Maia stopped, winced. I watched her try to swallow. I handed her the mug of tea. She panted 'thanks' and sipped. She handed the mug back to me, shut her eyes and settled back. I felt her body shake next to mine.

I whispered, "Are you alright?"

She didn't answer for a long moment, then, "It's fucking brutal." She licked her parched lips, "Fucking brutal."

I asked if there was anything I could do. She shook her head 'no'. I leaned into her body slightly and took her cold hand. I shut my eyes and vaguely prayed for her. The woodstove chuffed. I listened to Maia's breathing.

Minutes later, she spoke in fragments, "It didn't last long—-he got laid off. They all did. We had a place together by then. He got…mean, was drinking. Too much time on his hands — I got pregnant. I *wanted* the baby." She paused. "That pissed him off. We decided…*he* decided we should move to Vermont…his family. They'd help us. He could get a job at some relative's dairy farm. Better than being a bum in Pittsburg, he said. Raise the kid right, he said. He had family —it made sense."

I could barely hear her and had to lean in closer.

Very faintly, "What else could I do?" Her body quaked. She grabbed my hand with a sudden, fierce strength. She moaned. Then a small yelp. I panicked. She slowly released her grip. I stroked her hand, her wrist. I didn't know anything.

I asked if it was always like this. She didn't answer. Desperate, I asked if there wasn't something she could take that would help, something for the pain. I was thinking morphine; didn't they give morphine or something to people who were in this bad shape? She turned her head, not lifting it from the pillow, her brown eyes open, looking into mine. "I'm saving it."

Fuck no! I knew what she meant!

"Maybe you can help me" Her eyes steeled, flashed, hard on me, "If the time comes." She lashed me to her fate, to a point in time that would arrive. I went cold. "Don't worry." She rubbed her dry palm against the back of my hand.

She glanced away, suggested I put some more wood in the stove. I carefully pulled away. How long had I been in that bed? This night existed outside of time. I touched Maia's cheek with my fingertips, and my heart flew open. Everything it contained flowed over her like a stream of light. I whispered, "I love you." Her beautiful brown eyes smiled. That was why I was there, to say those words in that moment.

As I shut the stove door, I heard Maia speak, "You're lovely." Her voice sounded stronger. I asked if there was anything she wanted and she said no. I stood at the foot of the bed.

"Please come back." She pushed the covers down a bit. I heard her voice inside me say *don't worry.* I lowered myself back into bed, took her hand and settled my body next to hers. I brought her my warmth and she thanked me. The stove's heat pushed back against the chill. I laid my arm over her and we nestled.

A few minutes passed before she said, "I need to finish."

I nodded.

"We moved here, to this cabin, when I was seven months pregnant. Doug worked at his uncle's farm. He changed, though. He wasn't fun anymore. I got to know his family. They were quiet, took their time getting to know a person. Doug was working a lot. I was alone most days up here and without a second car. Rita started coming around with her kids. She'd bring me into town. He was always on me if I spent any money, said we had to save up for the hospital." Maia winced, her body wracked. She breathed raggedly. She bit off, "Back then I wished I wasn't here, wished I had someone who would..."

My stomach dropped at her recalled desperation. While she was here, pregnant and alone, my life couldn't have been better in San Francisco. I pulled the cuff of my sleeve over my palm and swabbed at my tears. Maia stayed quiet for a long while. Her body relaxed. I thought she may have slipped to sleep. I watched her bare-boned chest haltingly rise and sink with each breath.

She finally stirred, opened her drifting eyes, "I'm blessed. My beautiful Luke. He was only three when I got sick." She closed her eyes, "He'll only remember me as sick."

I took her hand.

"He doesn't know me. He'll need to forget me."

I told her I disagreed, that he'd need to remember her.

Silence.

She said, "Doug might not be too helpful that way. He didn't take too many pictures."

I asked her if she had any photographs of her and Luke, of the three of them together. There was a camera somewhere with pictures on the card. They had never been downloaded. She thought the camera might be in her bedroom, maybe in the nightstand by the bed. I promised I would find it and make copies of the pictures for Luke.

"Where's Doug?" I asked gently.

Maia squeezed my hand, I felt sheets of pain rippling through her. She licked her lips, "He'll be here. Maybe tomorrow. He's on his way from North Dakota, the oil fields."

I asked how long he had been out there.

She answered most of the past two years, he came back a couple weeks a year. "He sends money for me and Luke. Pays Rita some to help me out." Her voice went faint, "I don't know how we'd do it if he wasn't making good money."

The night's cold pressed against us. I asked Maia if she wanted me to find her camera so we could look at pictures together. She nodded and smiled. "I have to pee."

I helped wrap her in the afghan. Holding my arm, she slowly shuffled to the bathroom. "This'll get me going." She joked. The bathroom was cleaner than I thought it would be, and I credited Rita. I stood by. As Maia lifted the hem of her oversized t-shirt, I noticed her emaciated calves and thighs. "You can leave now. Some privacy, please." She smiled awkwardly.

I left to find the camera, called over my shoulder, "Let me know if you need any help." My words sounded insane, desperate. I found it and as we returned to the bed, Maia squeezed my arm, "I'm glad you're here, Tom"

We settled back in under the covers. I asked if she was left alone nights. She said a hospice worker, a nice older woman would come in the evenings. She added, "But tonight is different."

We spent a long time looking at the saved pictures through the beat up Canon's small screen: Birthdays, Christmases, Easters, Halloweens, scenes at a lake, and scenes in the snow. Luke as a baby; bundled, naked, smiling, scowling. Luke in Maia's arms, tucked beneath her chin, Maia smiling inwardly. Luke as a toddler; holding on to table edges, reaching for cake, holding Maia's hand, holding Doug's. Party pictures with Doug's relatives. Maia explained people, places. I spotted a younger Rita in a few shots. Maia stopped at a picture of Doug looking sternly at the camera, holding his boy on his shoulder, both squinting into the sunlight with the same expression. In the photos following Luke's toddler years, Maia rarely appeared.

When she did, she seemed to be a shadow of herself. I could make out the pain in her eyes. She offered fewer explanations of the scenes or the occasions, her voice trailing off.

Luke's face was so much like Doug's, but he had Maia's warm brown eyes. It seemed his eyes appeared frightened at times, even while he laughed on camera. I may have been imagining that. What did he know? Had he known his mother was so sick? Had he worried his father wouldn't return when he was gone for long stretches? How tense were things between Maia and Doug? What had he seen? How much had he felt? When did he become a part of Rita's family and leave his mother to her dying? I pressed my lips together. I clamped my eyes against the crushing images. Maia had stopped talking.

"Luke is beautiful. I'm going to make sure he gets these."

Through my exhaustion, I thought — *not enough.* "I'm going to make copies of pictures I have of you from San Francisco." She squeezed my hand. We held tight. I felt the cancer stalking her. I felt — *not enough.* I added, "I'll tell him all about you, how beautiful you were, and funny, and how you loved him so very much. I'll tell him stories." Instinctively, I knew Doug would not. I understood he had already put memory of her to rest, moved on. But a child needs the memory of his mother, I thought. You lose that connection and your soul drifts. Maia nodded slightly. I felt her deep appreciation.

At that moment I decided I would contact Luke at least once a year, around the time of Maia's birthday, and tell him stories about his mother. I still had her letters. I asked her if she had any pictures or mementoes she wanted me to share with Luke. She answered that there was a shoebox on the shelf in the bedroom closet she wanted me to have and to share with Luke. She pressed into me, rested her head against my chest.

I was in the strange twilit world between wakefulness and sleep, breathing the air that contained us, together; images of her life, real and imagined, were streaming over my eyelids when Maia spoke, "It's almost dawn. I think I want to end like this."

"What do you mean?"

"Like this, *happy*."

I couldn't look at her, "Doug will be here soon."

I felt her watching me, "He doesn't want to be here. His eyes will be lying even if he doesn't say a word. I don't think I want to see his eyes like that, before I go."

"Luke?"

"We had a wonderful day yesterday, before you came. We played Parcheesi in the morning with his cousins, made popcorn, got silly and laughed a lot. Real kid laughter. That's what I want for my last memory of him." She shut her eyes, "That's what I want his last memory of me to be." She pressed her lips together, then. "He doesn't need to be here when I leave. I don't want him to see me... They've been talking about putting me on one of those drips soon. I don't want that — Luke doesn't need — that."

I held back a painful sob.

"There's a bottle of pills on the shelf, near the tea. And there's a yogurt container with pills, in the back of the freezer. Nobody knows." She was staring at me hard. "Please bring them to me with a glass of water, Tom. Then tell me some stories — to remember in my dreams." She shut her eyes. We were lulled into silence. "I'm tired."

I left the bed to get the pills and water. I noticed the sky lighten outside the window over the sink and the ridgeline taking shape in the soft eastern glow. I returned to her bed. Stood by her side, watched as she clenched against her agony. "Maia." She opened her brown eyes, pleadingly. I handed her the first two pills and a short glass of water. She swallowed. Her expression told me to continue. I handed her one pill at a time until they were all gone. She never refused the next. I don't know how many she took — I didn't want to know. With the last pill, she drained the glass. Her eyes were surprisingly warm, grateful. She asked me to make us both a cup of tea.

I watched the sky's pink turn blue and I prepared tea. It was going to be a clear day. When I returned to the bed with the mugs, Maia didn't open her eyes. She was breathing evenly. Perhaps she sensed my return. Her skin was smooth. I lay beside her, atop the covers, put my mouth close to her ear, and began the story of the first time we met. How I saw her from across a patio on a summer evening scented with fresh cut grass and eucalyptus. How I heard her laugh, and how she was the most beautiful woman I had ever seen. How the sun had caught her hair. I told her how there was nothing in the world I wanted more than to be beside her. I told her how I was walking inches off of the ground and that it seemed like an eternity for me to reach her. I told her how, when we were together, side by side that evening, it was as if we had been beside each other our entire lives; how we smoothly folded into each other; how I smelled her and tasted her on the slight breeze; how the sun heated her skin so that I felt it inches away, and how our conversation brought us even closer. I told her how her words landed like a gentle rain — they carried her kindness to me. She had spoken her heart to me, and I had touched her hand. I told her that I still remembered her touch, both cool and sun warmed at the same time; that I had looked down at our hands, noticed them touching, and knew that I would remember the sight of them forever. I asked Maia if she remembered me raising her fingers to my lips and kissing them. I told her I remembered being caught in the tenderness of her brown eyes as I kissed her fingers, swimming in love, in that California evening.

I heard the breath catch in Maia's throat. I was holding her hand as she shook free. I felt her leave. I heard the rattle in the back of her throat. I pressed her hand to my lips and prayed, "I hope you are loved forever Maia."

Author's Bio:

Ea Burke lives in southern Vermont where he has raised a family and has practiced law in a solo practice for over thirty years. He was born, raised and educated in Philadelphia, with its trenchant wisdom. From there he explored a variety of lives in Boulder, Maui, San Francisco, Seattle, Akutan and Bristol Bay, Alaska before settling down in his heartland, Vermont. Upon graduating from Vermont Law School , Ea immediately took to representing people with legal needs that have run from the mundane to the desperate and tragic.

Ea's poetry has been published in a number of literary journals and poetry collections over the years, most recently Ginosko Literary Journal, Vol. 20, Winter 2017-2018; PoemCity 2017, 2018 and 2019; and honored with third place recognition in The Putney Mountain Poetry Contest, 2018. Ea's novel, Christine, Released will be published by Running Wild Press.

Faith Healing for Pessimists

By Anastasia Jill

I stood behind an old woman, raising my arms and singing along to the hip hop version of "Our God is an Awesome God." Our rehearsal space was smaller than a Polly Pocket nightmare, but in a three - floor hospital, with more patients than rooms, we had little choice than to rehearse in the abandoned rec room. I danced, bumped into other women and men, tried not to wipe out over the old foosball table.

The doors were wide open and broadcasting Christian music into the hallway. No one particularly minded the music, not the patients, nor the other employees. The medical center I worked at was owned by Adventists and once a month, we put on a show for the patients. Being the youngest in a chorus of old white people busting a jam, I couldn't help but feel more than a tad ridiculous.

We ran the number multiple times, until our too cheerful choir chaplain Kari said, "That's enough for today."

Most of the staff went back to work. I stayed behind to help clean. Kari stood by the door, with unenthusiastic nurses either ignoring or complaining to her. Once alone, I asked, "Why do you bother with any of this?"

She didn't say anything for a bit, as she watched the pendulum of my sweeping broom. When she did, all she could say was, "Take some Windex to the scuff marks on the floor."

"That's not my job," I said. "That's for housekeeping."

"Housekeeping isn't here to clean up after you."

That was fundamentally untrue, but I was in no mood to argue. Giving a salute, I got down on all fours and took to scrubbing the remnants of shoes and wheelchair marks from the unforgiving. She stood by and watched, a warm smile on her face. "Sometimes preaching doesn't reach people. A little energy and song goes a long way towards compassion."

"That's a bit of a reach."

"One way or another, we have their attention."

"We would anyways. It's the only hospital in town. People can either come here, or go home and die."

She pinched her brows in admonishment, but I paid her no mind. It was easier to stay compassionate, when things were in check. Within the last month, I'd lost my second job, drained all my savings and steered cautiously close to eviction. My boyfriend was prime to leave my life next, sick of the constant negativity. Kari told me to have faith. When things were crummy, faith meant nothing. Pessimism is what's hip these days, I had told her. She sighed and responded with, believe what you want, just cool it with the "death" talk around patients.

Gathering her belongings, she walked away, leaving me to put away the cleaning supplies. I turned the corner and nearly tripped on the guy standing there.

"Sorry," I grumbled.

"No, June. It's my fault," he conceded.

How did this guy know my name? I studied his small bloated frame. It took me a moment and that's when I recognized him as Kim Nguyen. We had had a few classes together at a community college, until he dropped out of sight.

"So sorry. It's just been a … sad day. Or at least, it was until I walked by the chapel and heard you all."

"Why are you wandering the halls?" I asked.

"The bus doesn't come for another hour, so I decided to try and find some food. Which I'm glad for, at least now." He gestured down the hall, in the direction of the chapel. "Who could be sad after hearing you rhyming for Jesus?"

"Yeah, it's a real crowd charmer." I brushed him aside and left the supplies for the janitor to collect. "What a hit, "I said sarcastically. "Really, where's my Grammy?" I was only half joking, but his laugh was full, real.

"So how've you been?" He asked.

"Okay, I guess."

"Are you a doctor now or something?"

"I'm a medical receptionist, which is a fancy way of saying I give tours and verify social security cards." Looking him up and down, I crossed my arms and stood against the wall. "You never answered my question. Why are you here? Visiting a relative or something like that?"

"Something like that." He shrugged. "Uh … you know. Just chilling."

"In a hospital?"

"Is that not where the youth chill these days?"

It was my turn to laugh, the first real one in a while. Moments later, the pager in my pocket went off. "I have to get back to work."

"What time do you get off work?"

"Three – thirty. Why?"

"Want to meet up, bust a jam, or grab some lunch? There's a new barbeque place I've been meaning to try. It's only up the street."

I mentioned there was a guy in the picture to which he replied, "Aren't you allowed to catch up with old classmates?"

When I tensed, he reached for my shoulder and gave it a congenial squeeze. "Relax. I'm just … stuck here for a bit and relieved to see someone my own age."

Panicking again, I told him my wallet was empty. It didn't seem to faze him.

"Okay. My treat." He smiled.

Figuring the afternoon offered nothing else, I agreed When the conversation was over, I rushed back down the hall, turning to watch him as I walked away. He realized I was staring and gave a wave. I waved back then went on my way.

The afternoon spaced itself between patients, the monotony broken up by the occasional fractured bone or unidentified pain. When it was time to punch out, I was quick to clean up my desk, procure my purse from the back of my chair, and take the elevator down to the bottom floor. I found my van and practically sped down the road to meet Kim.

I saw him waiting outside a shanty of a restaurant; the building was painted white and offered mostly outdoor seating. He looked uncomfortable in the midst of a large crowd, sitting with Styrofoam boxes in his hands. He greeted me and apologized. "They were closing for lunch and I wanted to make sure we got something."

I'd barely eaten in a week and had no disputes in telling him, "This is fine, really. Thank you." He put a container in my hand, which I opened to find a serving of mac and cheese, some baked beans, and a few chicken wings slathered in an unidentifiable, but savory looking sauce.

"Do you want to sit here or … there's more seating in the back."

I took a hearty bite of my slop before answering, "Sounds good to me. Lead the way."

I shoveled in bits of the food, as we ambled behind the restaurant to find the empty tables. Quaint patches of grass bore dandelions too yellow to grant wishes. We sat on the rusted chairs, and set the containers on the hole-covered table before eating again.

Well, I ate again. His food sat there, barely touched, his hands looked paler than the plastic fork. I didn't say anything, thinking it rude to comment on eating habits.

He faced me and asked, "When's the main performance?"

"Next Sunday, right after lunch." I said with a mouthful of beans. "High point of our day. If you're not a doctor or nurse, attendance is mandatory."

He inched closer to me. "Even for the patients?"

"If you want your medication, it is."

We both laughed at my joke even though I wasn't trying to be funny.

"I can't tell if you're serious about the music being good, but thanks regardless," I said.

It seemed he needed a reason to smile. The tug in his voice betrayed his jubilant stance.

"You're not here visiting family, are you?" I asked.

He scooted away. "No. I was brought in yesterday and I left today."

He must have come gone to ER, because he hadn't checked in or out from the front desk, I reasoned. "That's good they let you leave. So, you must be doing better then."

"In a manner of speaking, I guess."

Curiosity poked around my head, but I knew better than to ask questions. We barely knew each other, after all. He was a woebegone sight, with his eyes drained of color and his cheeks puffy, at closer observation. Of course he was sick; that was obvious now that I knew. He had been released from the hospital. Clearly, he'd gotten help. Wanting to switch up the mood, I invited him to our performance on Sunday. This cheered him up for some reason, like he had a motive to make it that far.

Something caught in my throat. "You're dying, aren't you?" I asked gently.

He dropped his head. "Yes."

"What is it? What's wrong?"

His explanation was short. "Medulloblastoma. Posterior fossa. Stage four."

I was stunned into silence. Then, "The doctors here may be wacky and obsessed with Christian hip hop, but they're well trained and very smart. There's new technology and medial advancement. You'll be fine."

He shook his head. "I don't think so."

"Is there nothing they can do?"

Instead of answering my question, he stood up and offered me his container. "I'm not hungry." He placed it in my hands. "Can you drive me to the bus stop? I know it's not that far, but I'm a little tired."

I nodded and fell in step behind him.

"How long did the doctors give you?"

He shrugged. "I don't really know."

"What do you mean you don't know?"

"The odds of that aren't good, but they are great. Especially in adults."

His voice was calm as he spoke, "I don't know, June. I don't know."

Sidestepping him, I unlocked the driver's side door. "They must have told you something before you left."

He didn't turn around, but didn't hesitate in answering. "I left against doctor's orders, alright?" He was short of breath after the walk, so I helped him to the passenger side. Once in, I locked the door and turned the vents up. I never started the car. I just sat there with my hand on the key.

"The bus stop's just down the way." he said. "Seriously, I can walk."

"Doesn't look like you can make it that far." Once he composed himself, I gently asked what his prognosis might be.

"I'm not seeking medical treatment. I passed out at class last night and was unconscious, so they brought me here."

I tried retaining my sense of composure. "It's that bad that you just wanted to stop chemo?"

He shook his head. "No chemo, no radiation at all." Teeth ground into his lip. "My parents and I decided prayer and alternative medicine would be the best route."

"That's awful. And you went along with that?"

"My family thinks it's best."

"Kim, you're only in your twenties."

His eyes waxed defeat. "The pastor thought it was best. It's hard not to listen."

Before I knew it, I was crying for this boy I barely knew and the cancer eating his brain's opposition to logic. He tried to comfort me and I told him to stop.

"It's alright," he said. "Let's listen to some music."

He turned on the stereo in my car, the CD of Christian music playing loudly in our ears. His leftover food sat in my lap, and the sky turned dark with late afternoon rain clouds. "What can I do to change your mind?" I asked him.

"Nothing. What's done is done."

The music cut short as the CD skipped.

"I feel like I should do something for you." I said.

"There's nothing you can do…" He paused. "God will take me as far as He wants me." His voice was flat.

I wrapped my hand around his and held it over the console. "Was there something that could have been done sooner?"

"My parents pulled medical treatment right after my diagnosis. Maybe so, maybe not. It was a futile effort."

His clammy hand chilled my bones. “If it makes you feel better, I haven’t suffered.”

I opened an eye in his direction. “But you’re still going to die.”

“No one knows that, but God.”

It was too overcast to tell if the sun set or not, but he let go of me and I settled back into

the present. The song *Awesome God* was playing. I had put that disc on in the morning for my ride to work. The chorus sounded bitter and bright as the woman on the track sang, “… *He reigns with wisdom, power and love, our God is an awesome God!*”

“It’s scary, but I have faith. And this afternoon with you—-may not seem like it, but it was

to get reacquainted.” Opening the door, he stepped out of my yellow van. “I’ll see you Sunday afternoon, breaking a move?”

I laughed through my plucked grief. “That’s busting a move.”

“Regardless.” He shut the door tight. Nodding through the open window, he dabbed his eyes before he walked away and called out, “It was nice to see you again, June!”

“Yeah, I guess.”

His kindness foraged optimism from the raw darkness of the situation. For a moment, I believed I would see him. I knew he’d get better. I found out about Kim a few days later, when he was in fact deceased.

Kim’s death made the local news. He had passed away while at a bus stop near his home. Winter Park was a small community, where any little thing made the news. My head was in a fog, but from the article and linked video posted to Facebook, I learned he had collapsed onto the concrete. Someone had called an ambulance, but he was pronounced dead on arrival. After learning of the news, I skipped part of my afternoon shift and sat on the passenger side of my van. Just a few days ago he had sat here, offering me his food and justifying the prayer and quasi-wisdom that would leave him for dead. Shaking against the leather, I ran my hand over the dashboard, where most of my trash remained, including the empty Styrofoam container.

My fist clenched against my thigh, knowing what Kim would say if he were here. Nothing serious, nothing pokey. He'd remind me that I had a performance at four. The clock read 3:45. There was still time to afford others the kindness Kim afforded to me. Crying again, I wanted nothing more than to go home. Instead, I stepped out and went back inside, ready to sing at the top of my lungs.

Author's Bio:

Anastasia Jill is a queer writer living in the South. Her work has been nominated for Best of the Net and Best Small Fiction Anthology and has been featured with Poets.org, Lunch Ticket, FIVE:2:ONE, apt, Anomaly Literary Journal, 2River, Gertrude Press, Minola Review, and more.

Final Exit

By Abdullah Aljumah

The fact that Salwa was acutely anemic and chronically ill with sickle cell disease made it very hard on her family members to break to her the news of her husband's death. They couldn't afford to lose her, too.

The news of his death came via a phone call past midnight, from her brother-in law, who had been deployed in Jubail, during the first Gulf war, around two hundred kilometers away from the Saudi-Kuwaiti border. He had received the news via a phone call from a sergeant deployed in Khafji city close to Kuwait, asking if the deceased was his relative. He then called another colleague, deployed in the same area, to inquire about the matter, who confirmed the tragic news that, Hassan, indeed, had passed away.

The task of breaking the news was assigned to her older sister, Rehab, who reached Salwa's house early in the morning. She attempted to explain to her, in peculiar broken sentences, with tears running down her cheeks that it was liable to have happened anytime. Salwa took the news like any wife would. She fell to her knees, pulled her hair and tore up her clothes. She screamed, wailed, and lamented her loss. When her grief finally took its toll on her, she stopped. She grabbed her blue-eyed toddler and ran into her bedroom.

There, she locked herself inside and mourned her prearranged marriage and unfulfilled life with Hassan. She lay down in her bed, motionless, with closed eyes in reverie. She thought of sweet Alabama, where her deceased husband had received his overseas military training four years ago. Though she had spent only two years there, she quite clearly remembered every single detail of it. She thought back on the days she had spent wandering throughout the state's natural wonders and exploring its hidden gems. She pictured the free-flowing Cahaba scenic river and its breathtaking lilies. In her contemplation, she recalled the fatal attraction that took place, while walking around Cahaba farmer's market. That's where she had met Daniel, the blue-eyed florist selling freshly-cut camellia flowers. As the young American man handed her the bouquet of pink and red flowers, their hands touched and flames of desire had danced up her arm, warming the depth of her heart. Thoughts of those flowers conjured long-forgotten memories of him. The pink flowers infused a passion and deep longing she innately felt she could now be able to fulfill. The red flowers ignited a previously burnt out flame in her heart that was now renewed. The heart-stopping moments of their onetime forbidden love affair danced in her thoughts. Then she sat on the edge of her bed by the nightstand and pulled out a picture of her toddler holding a plastic bouquet of similar flowers. There, now feeling exhilarated with hope, the white flowers completed the picture depicted in her mind with perfect adoration.

As her toddler slept, Salwa walked to her full-length mirror and gazed at herself. Her once barely-visible pupils slowly came to life. Being quite young and beautiful, she breathed with a deep sigh and felt her bosom rise up and down impulsively. She tucked loose strands of her dark hair behind her right ear. Tucking her hair was a habitual sign of relief. She used to feel trapped, but now she felt free. Her toddler woke up from his nap, whining. His mesmerizing eyes sparkled. He had the same unmistakably distinctive blue eyes, which had created such uncertainty among Salwa's in-laws.

She clutched him close to her chest, whispered in his ear, "We're gonna go see daddy."

She carefully opened the drawer again and snatched her passport. She booked herself and their own son on the earliest flight she could find, a one-way ticket to sweet Alabama, assuring herself it would be a final exit from her homeland, with no turning back.

A few days later, Salwa's mom walked into her daughter's empty bedroom and sat on the edge of the bed by the nightstand. She glanced around, searched for an answer to her daughter's impulsive and unthinking departure. "It must be the black magic workings of her husband's family," she concluded as she shed her dearest tears.

On the Hassawi Sparrow

By Abdullah Aljumah

A gentle breeze rustled through the regimented stillness of evergreen palm leaves. Then, on its thorny twig, there was a flicker of color and a whisper of movement as a tiny, but inviting creature suddenly moved, and rays of scattered sunlight cascaded from two grey brown pairs of shiny wings. on a plump, bright brown body, and from a pair of round black eyes as fierce as those of the *Hassawi* sparrow.

Known in *Al-Mubarraz* as *Um Juffayyer*, but in villages surrounding *Al-Ahsa* as *Um Ozeir* was this small low-flying sparrow. I owed this majestic sparrow debts of gratitude. It brightened my life and honed my hunting ability. This glorious sparrow had been the first bird I caught with my slingshot.

One Friday morning, I spotted *Um Juffayyer* flying low in *Al-Barrak* farm. I followed it. It hovered nearby and perched on a pomegranate tree. I tiptoed closer, pointing my slingshot towards the bird and stretched my left arm as far as I could. I shot, but missed. It swiftly bristled and flew to a mulberry tree nearby. I grabbed another fat, sharp and pointy stone from my right pocket, twice bigger than the size of the poor sparrow's head. Taking a step closer, I shot my deadly weapon. Alas! I missed again. It flew to a palm tree nearby just right above my head. I observed the tree for a few moments, searching for my prey. A breezy wind exposed the fierce eyes of the sparrow.

There it stood, regally around four meters high away from me. I shot. The fat stone flew off my slingshot; feathers scattered in the air, and on the ground tumbled down the majestic sparrow. "I hit it," I screamed. I ran, yelling, "I hit it. I caught a bird!" I screamed at the top of my head. I jumped and wiggled my arms, laughing and dancing. I grabbed the poor bird in my hand and took off, heading home to deliver my mom the news of my harvest.

Laughs echoed in the distance, "Saloom just caught *Um Juffayyer*," I heard a familiar voice. "With all that screaming, I thought you'd caught a falcon," he continued.

I froze. It was Ammar with a wide smirk on his face. I didn't dare say a thing. I just limped past him as he kicked at me. I took off running home with the little dead sparrow cradled in my hands.

Exposed

By Abdullah Aljumah

An arm length away from the floor hangs his garb. His long beard falls down, short of his navel. He goes to bed overwhelmed with worry and wakes up totally lost in an ocean deep of desires and conflicts, buried underneath. He often has vague dreams, dreams of worldly ambitions with bleary colors. Wherever he goes, he puts on his widely respected — yet highly horrifying — short *thobe*. His intensive, demanding, loud supplications and prayers in the mosque are about to enrage Allah. He sometimes entertains doubts about the existence of Him, which he swiftly disqualifies, but soon they insist on recurring in the folds of his subconscious mind.

He comes closer to a mirror and, as he sees his short traditional clothing, as opposed to his long beard, reflected in the mirror, he feels a deep sorrow in his heart. He recalls his youth, which was sucked up by his horrifying beard and clothes. He starts combing his long, salt and pepper beard. The thick gray hair intensifies year after year and it reminds him of elderliness and wilt. He grew his beard for so many years and it has now reached the middle of his broad chest.

***

While passing in his luxurious van last night, he caught a glimpse of a clean-shaven chap walking on the side of the road. "That handsome young man needs enlightenment," he whispered to himself. "That's my job." He pulled over and took fast steps towards the young man. As soon as he approached, he took notice of the attractive man's creamy-white hand. Warm passion engulfed the religious old man as they shook hands. A solemn, but respectful dialog went on between them. The young man told him stories gleaned from the nectar of youth and after a long talk, they told one another about the principles of their life.

Before they parted, the young man said, "Sorry, *ya sheikh*, I'd like to ask you a personal question, but I am embarrassed towards your highly dignified person."

The *muttawa* replied, "Sure, my son. I am all ears."

The young man faked an embarrassment, but he was ready for such an encounter and threw out his question, "I wonder where you position your long beard when you go to bed. Do you position it on top of the quilt or under it?"

"And why do you ask such a question?"

"In fact I imagined myself wearing such a long beard and I found myself perplexed to answer the same question. So, I wanted to ask you. *Ya sheikh*, I know how naive such a question could be and I'm sorry if I've intruded on your privacy, but I also know how much tolerance, forgiveness and good-heartedness you possess and won't mind such a private question. Actually, I'd like to know where all religious men, such as yourself, position their long beards when they lie in bed and in a deep sleep."

After a long pause, the *muttawa* replied, "In fact, I don't know where I position my beard during sleep. I have never thought about it to say the least. I sometimes position it on the quilt and at other times under it." Then, smiling he asked, "But why do you ask me this specific question?"

"The truth is it's just a question, a sort of curiosity. That's all."

Nodding his head, the *muttawa* continued, "Anyway, I'll tell you tomorrow where I position my beard."

The young man stuttered, then remarked, "Remember this well, *ya sheikh*, do not forget where you set your beard before you succumb to sleep?"

"I will remember and I will tell you tomorrow where I position it. I'll meet you at the cafe down the corner of the street. Right after *Maghrib* prayer."

***

In the evening, the *muttawa* performed his ablution and his usual prayer and when it was time to sleep, he remembered the nice-looking man's question. He lay in bed, covered himself well and took no notice of his second wife sleeping beside him. In the beginning, he positioned his beard under the quilt, but he was quickly bored with it and positioned it on the quilt, imagining the latter position provided further comfort for him. Moments later, he felt its current position didn't provide the comfort he needed and placed it, instead, under the quilt. His focus intensified on its position: under the quilt or on it. Then, he repositioned it on the quilt and under the quilt, alternating a dozen of times 'till he reached a point where he couldn't sleep. He confined his thinking to his beard and started whispering to himself, "In fact, the good-looking man was right to be perplexed about where he'd position his imagined beard." The attractive man's face glowed vividly in the vision of the sheikh's subconscious desires.

The *muttawa* stroked his beard several times, got up, walked to the mirror, and began staring at his face. His eyes were bloodshot, sweat running down his forehead. He felt a strange itching in his chin. He rubbed his chin, but he momentarily felt he couldn't rub it well. He found himself pacing the bedroom for a long time. He headed to the bathroom. The young man's question was still rolling in his head. Whispering, he echoed the nice-looking man's question; do not forget to tell me where you will position your beard before you go to sleep!

He felt utter confusion. He shook his head rhythmically up and down, as if to nod and muttered inaudible words while addressing himself. He took off his clothes and began to bathe with lukewarm water. He thought the shower would give him a state of relaxation and eventually he'd surrender to sleep. Instead, he was energized and perked up. He became obsessed with looking in the mirror at his naked body, and then he muttered, "Where is that frightening *thobe*? Oh, my body, how grieved, under the clothes of chastity!"

The water droplets started falling down his long beard. He remembered his past youth, how he used to shave daily to appear presentable. Questions hailed down on him from each and every part of his past, and he felt he was swinging between the spiritual worlds and the physical one. He imagined that the physical propensity sometimes swayed away his spiritual inclinations.

He was perplexed and disoriented by thoughts of the young man. He shook his head and tried to ponder in metaphysics. But, metaphysics seemed to him an absolute jelly and he could not find a well-defined path for the devilish thoughts he'd got thrown into. He returned to his bed, his head full of unanswered questions. He curled up under the quilt. He was about to sleep, but the young man's question was still vivid in his memory, and soon the puzzling journey began taking over again! Whenever he positioned his beard under or on the quilt, he felt the need to reposition it. And as such confusion threw him in a dark maze; his eyelids did not find a way to sleep. Then he whispered to himself, "What calamity overcame me with such a coincidental meeting with this attractive man!"

He began conversing with himself in a wandering bafflement. The young man's question occupied the largest part of the befuddling puzzle. Insomnia besieged him from every side and he began turning in his bed for hours. Then, at last, he surrendered to sleep — exposed!

The next morning, he lazily got up from his bed, and he never knew where he had positioned his beard during his sleep. The only thing he knew, he was sleepless and the handsome man's face lingered in his mind.

Author's Bio:

Abdullah Aljumah is bilingual and bicultural. He received his Master's degree in Linguistics from Eastern Michigan University sponsored by the Fulbright program. He works as an Instructional Supervisor for the General Education Department of the Royal Commission. He writes short stories revolving around religious hypocrisy, religious conflicts, forced marriages as well as childhood experience.

Past Titles

Running Wild Stories Anthology, Volume 1
Running Wild Anthology of Novellas, Volume 1
Jersey Diner by Lisa Diane Kastner
Magic Forgotten by Jack Hillman
The Kidnapped by Dwight L. Wilson
Running Wild Stories Anthology, Volume 2
Running Wild Novella Anthology, Volume 2, Part 1
Running Wild Novella Anthology, Volume 2, Part 2
Running Wild's Best of 2017, AWP Special Edition
Running Wild's Best of 2018
Build Your Music Career From Scratch, Second Edition by Andrae Alexander
Writers Resist: Anthology 2018 with featured editors Sara Marchant and Kit-Bacon Gressitt
Magic Forbidden by Jack Hillman
Frontal Matter: Glue Gone Wild by Suzanne Samples
Mickey: The Giveaway Boy by Robert M. Shafer
Dark Corners by Reuben "Tihi" Hayslett
The Resistors by Dwight L. Wilson

Upcoming Titles

Running Wild Stories Anthology, Volume 3, Book 1
Running Wild Stories Anthology, Volume 3, Book 2
Running Wild Stories Anthology, Volume 3, Book 3
Open My Eyes by Tommy Hahn
Legendary by Amelia Kibbie
Running Wild Press, Best of 2018
Running Wild Anthology of Stories, Volume 4
Christine, Released by E. Burke

Running Wild Press publishes stories that cross genres with great stories and writing. Our team consists of:

Lisa Diane Kastner, Founder and Executive Editor
Barbara Lockwood, Editor
Cecile Sarruf, Editor
Peter Wright, Editor
Piper Daniels, Editor
Benjamin White, Editor
Andrew DiPrinzio, Editor
Amrita Raman, Operations Manager
Lisa Montagne, Director of Education

Learn more about us and our stories at www.runningwildpress.com

Loved this story and want more? Follow us at
www.runningwildpress.com, www.facebook.com/runningwildpress,
on Twitter @lisadkastner @JadeBlackwater @RunWildBooks

CPSIA information can be obtained
at www.ICGtesting.com
Printed in the USA
BVHW070813260919
559450BV00006B/27/P

9 781947 041301